Lois McMaster Bujold

This special signed edition is limited to 1250 numbered copies.

This is copy **801**.

Penric and the BANDIT

A PENRIC & DESDEMONA
NOVELLA IN THE WORLD OF
THE FIVE GODS

Lois McMaster Bujold

SUBTERRANEAN PRESS 2025

Penric and the Bandit
Copyright © 2024 by Lois McMaster Bujold.
All rights reserved.

Dust jacket illustration Copyright © 2025 by Lauren Saint-Onge.
All rights reserved.

Interior design Copyright © 2025 by Desert Isle Design, LLC.
All rights reserved.

First Hardcover Edition

ISBN
978-1-64524-272-7

Subterranean Press
PO Box 190106
Burton, MI 48519

subterraneanpress.com

Manufactured in the United States of America

THE FLAXEN-HAIRED YOUNG man looked out of place in this grubby taverna. Also a bit lost? Roz studied him, matching him up with the hardy horse stabled a while ago with the village blacksmith, who provided that service for the few travelers staying the night in one of the tiny upstairs chambers here. Roz was another such. The horse's tack had been good quality, if not new. Its owner had paid coin up front for board for both himself and his beast. He wasn't flaunting the fatness of his purse, but he also hadn't tried to bargain the prices down. *He doesn't have to be rich. Just richer than me.* Which wasn't hard, these days.

The stranger was not from anywhere around here, that was certain. Startlingly pale skin flushed with sunburn, gold-blond hair in a braided queue halfway down his back, lanky build: in his army days, Roz had glimpsed a few like-hued fellows at the river port city in Grabyat, and been told they were merchant traders from the far south. The fabled ice islands were also noted for sea pirates, but Roz doubted this one had ever hauled a rope or swung a battle axe in his short life. Or any other kind of axe. He wore ordinary tunic and trousers, well made; excellent riding boots, like the tack. Promising...

Goldie pulled a tube of paper from his tunic and unrolled it on his table tucked against the wall. He unceremoniously trapped the curling edges with the pewter fork and spoon and clay beaker that awaited his meal, and scowled down at it. It seemed to Roz a prime chance to casually insert himself.

"Is that a map?" Roz asked, wandering over and producing a friendly curious smile.

The fellow looked up, swapping out his scowl for a smile of answering affability. "So it was claimed. It's been remarkably useless for finding my way about so far. I don't think this village is even on it." He turned it toward Roz for display.

Roz bent and peered. The writing was in some fancy Cedonian script, which he could recognize but not read. The fellow's speech, too, was Cedonian—not the dialect of south Grabyat where Roz had grown up, nor that of the neighboring mountain district of Oxousa in Trigonie where this village lay,

Penric and the BANDIT

but clear-spoken enough that Roz had little trouble making out his words. Roz sneaked a peek at his hands, always telling. Long fingers ink-stained, none missing. No laborer, this. A scribe?

"I see your problem," said Roz, pretending to read. The map showed roads and rivers, or more likely trails and streams, with mountains sketched-in that seemed more artistic than realistic. Its area did not seem large. "What are you looking for, if not this village? Ah—may I?" Roz gestured at the opposite chair, and with a wave of his hand Goldie invited him to seat himself.

"Are you a local man?" asked the fellow.

"Not from here, no. But I've knocked around Oxousa for the past few years." And while implying expertise, he'd have to be careful not to tempt the next obvious question, *Doing what?*

An inky finger tapped a tiny pentagon drawn on the map. "I seek a mountain temple. Very high up, by the description. It might be overdramatic to call it *lost*, but certainly abandoned long ago."

Roz's brows flicked up. *Now, what would he want with such a thing?* "There are temples in Oxousa aplenty, but not many abandoned. And most are in towns, to serve the people. Abandoned hill forts, now, there are any number of those." He and his comrades had holed up in a few, in worser days.

Goldie shook his head. "Those tend to be located along main routes, river or road, or by settlements. Or passes, sometimes."

For the traffic, yes, ideal.

"This place was more reclusive, I understand. Deliberately. Possibly hoping to avoid the several wars that have washed over the region in the past. Military protection can turn to military looting at the loss of a battle."

So true. "Was this temple ever attacked?"

"My sources didn't say anything about its ever being sacked. The failure of a spring was mentioned. Also a plague or two. Such remote refuges tend to avoid contagions, but once they do get in, they race through the residents. Who might simply have grown too few to maintain the place." The fellow's unusual blue eyes narrowed. "One might tell something by examining the ruins. Different things get left, depending on the reasons for flight. Sacking is actually more likely to miss valuable items than a studied removal."

The fellow and his bad map grew abruptly *far* more interesting. "Do you seek something valuable left there?"

Penric and the BANDIT

"Valuable to me, maybe. Or not. I thought it worth a look."

"A long way to ride, for a thin chance."

A quirky smile twitched the man's lips. "I have a peculiar relationship with chance. And I was due a little holiday."

Poor men did not get *holidays*. Nor the spare funds to jaunt about for weeks doing no work. "What's the name of the place? I may have heard of it."

"The Seminary of Gramez. Or possibly also the Hermitage of the Blessed Aziji. The first name might have come from village or township or patron. The second was a person, but still, associated."

Goldie was a gormless fool, to give up those identifiers so easily to a chance-met stranger at an inn. Not a point against him, for Roz's purposes. But since Roz did not recognize the names, maybe not such a blunder after all. He shook his head in unfeigned regret.

"Ah," said Goldie. "No surprise I'm not lucky on the first try. It will probably take five." He tapped the back of his thumb to his lips, twice, a gesture of the fifth god whose odd blessings most prudent men did not invoke, so he might be more frustrated than he looked. "I'm Pen, by the way. Short for Penric. Canton name, to save you asking. And yourself?"

The Cantons were supposed to be mountain country somewhere south of Adria and Carpagamo, Roz thought. Not quite as far as the ice islands, then. "Roz. Short for Rozak, which is short for Rozakajin." His real name, for a change—it had been a while since he'd deployed it in his round of aliases, so likely safe.

"And which do you prefer?"

"Roz. I was Rozak in the army, which left me a distaste for it."

"Which army?" asked Goldie-Pen brightly.

Ah, he shouldn't have mentioned that detail. But perhaps it would boost his plausibility as a guide-or-guard, an offer he might make shortly, depending. "Grabyat's."

"Fighting the Rusylli incursions, were you?"

"Mostly."

"Tough work, from what I've heard from another veteran."

Pen was more informed than most outlanders, then. Bastard's curse. "I don't much care to talk about it." Another overly true statement—he'd better limit those.

Penric and the BANDIT

But Pen merely nodded, and changed the subject. "And where are you bound now?"

"Berbak." The next town up this road worth the name. "I have a mule to sell. I think I can get a better price there."

Pen turned his map around and studied it again; his thumb came down on a spot on its edge. "Ah, there it is. I daresay you can." He cocked his head. "It looks like our ways may lie together, tomorrow. Care to join company?"

Roz tried not to smile too broadly. *Oh excellent.* That would give him another full day to sound out this traveler, gain his trust, and discover just what promise of treasure had brought him so neatly into Roz's ken. Without appearing overeager. "Yes, if it please you. This country is rife with bandits. Much safer not to travel alone."

"I never do, so yes." Pen nodded happily.

The taverna's girl arrived with their dinners, and Pen rolled up the intriguing map and tucked it away. Roasted mutton sausage, flatbread, goat cheese, cucumbers, onions, and olives, with a carafe of watered red wine to wash it down, occupied both men for a while.

After their table was cleared, Roz challenged Pen to a game of dice, for a test. The man was only willing to wager olive pits for counters, but Roz made sure his opponent won more than he lost. He was as cheerful about it as if it were coins. Not a natural gambler, then, despite his fresh-faced youth. Which made Roz increasingly curious about what Pen thought was hidden in that old temple, that was worth his exploratory chance-taking. Or maybe…he already knew?

Arriving at Berbak tomorrow night with a dupe and a direction was looking increasingly better than arriving there with a spare horse and gear to sell, even adding whatever coin this golden goose carried on his person. Also, ambushing an awake fit man, however trusting, in daylight was a hazardous task. It would be far easier to knife the man in his sleep in some night camp on the way back from his lost temple, when he would be carrying all he did now plus…what?

Confident in his new plan, Roz set the time for them to depart in the morning, and they bade each other cheery goodnights and went upstairs to bed.

Penric and the BANDIT

PENRIC WATCHED as the chamber door closed behind his dinner companion. And, it seemed, future road companion. He entered his own room, just across the short hallway, prudently locking his door behind him. His saddlebags, left on the floor at the foot of his cot, appeared unrifled. So far.

This deception seems almost cruel, he remarked in their silent speech to his demon, Desdemona.

Which? His, or ours? she returned.

I was thinking ours, but I suppose his as well.

No almost about his. You did grasp that he is a trickster, yes?

I wasn't sure at first, but his sleight-of-hand with his loaded dice rather points to something of the sort. Subtle touch, letting us win. If he were a mere chance-met swindler, he should have tried harder to fleece us right then.

Difficult to do when you're only betting olive pits.

Well, yes. It seems he's looking ahead.

Baited with your map and your tale of treasure, I expect. You did that on purpose!

But he didn't have to bite...

Pen began to undress for bed, considering his new friend. Roz-Rozak-Rozakajin was a sturdy, if worn-looking, man of middle height. Typical peninsular coloration of the people of this region: warm skin darkened to walnut where the sun fell upon it, deep brown eyes, black hair cut too short to braid, curling loose around his head. His age was a puzzle. Not above thirty, certainly. Possibly some years less, depending on how hard a life he'd led— and if he'd been a foot soldier for Grabyat in the Rusylli campaigns, it might have been hard indeed. No particular clues in his clothing, which were the same tunic and trousers that any local might wear.

Any local workman, put in Des. *Which, granted, goes with the sun coloring.*

You'd think he would be better dressed if he were a bandit, Pen mused. *Those fellows tend to select among their spoils for the gaudiest garb.* Showing off, Pen supposed, though to whom he was not sure. Each other? Their camp followers?

He could be a clever advance scout for his friends, put in Des. *What are we to do if they turn up?*

Our sorcery can handle a few bandits. They can't be any harder than pirates.

Four, maybe. But what if it's forty? Your glib tongue would be no use if you can't survive long enough to speak. And I do not want *to be dumped into some grubby, ignorant hill bandit!*

Penric and the BANDIT

Pure spirit, the bodiless chaos demons of the fifth god could not survive in the world of matter without a creature of matter to support them, animal or human. As they never occupied lesser life, fish or insects or plants, Pen had long supposed there was some minimum level of energy and complexity required for this sustenance. When the death of their host evicted them, demons were compelled to jump to the next best living creature in range, always preferring to chain upwards from weaker to more powerful, less intelligent to greater. Through this process Desdemona herself had progressed through two animals and ten human women over two centuries of time, leaving her a very experienced demon indeed. With some very strong opinions about the matter.

Pen's grin flickered. He murmured aloud, "I shall try to keep you in your current congenial abode."

You'd better! After a moment of brooding, she added slyly, *And while I have no doubt I could shortly ascend and walk our new body home to our wife, I can't think Nikys would appreciate the substitution.*

Now, there was a horrifying picture. After twenty-two years together, Pen supposed he should be used to his demon's bloody-mindedness, but Des could still surprise him. "Would it even be me, at that point? I thought my soul would go to our god, and what was left in you a mere imprint."

If you can't really tell the difference between, say, Learned Ruchia and her imprint in me—Ruchia being the only one of Des's prior riders Pen had met in the flesh, if only briefly as she lay dying on that far-off Canton roadside—*how should Nikys tell your imprint from you?*

"That is a very perturbing reflection, Des. Theologically and otherwise. It would be like having a ghost husband." Ghost widow? His beloved Nikys was a broad-minded woman, or she could not have encompassed her three-way marriage with her Temple sorcerer spouse and his resident demon, but there were some uncanny challenges he would rather not inflict upon her.

Good, grumped Des, as ever privy to his thoughts, though the reverse was not always the case. *Hold that resolution. That being so, what say we lose this Grabyat would-be trickster tomorrow?*

"Mm..." said Pen. "That seems premature. Even if he means to knife me in my sleep—"

To try to, growled Des.

Penric and the BANDIT

"He'd surely wait till after I locate whatever treasure he imagines I'm looking for in the lost temple."

I doubt he imagines the same sort of treasure you do. A snicker of irony from her which, to be fair, Penric shared.

"Likely not."

Are you planning to make game of the poor fellow?

"If so, it could be a game with a serious prize. As a learned divine of the Bastard's Order, my mandate of care does include the souls of thieves."

So, what, Learned, you want to run him in Penric-circles till he reforms of sheer exhaustion?

"Would it amuse you to watch?"

...Yes, she admitted grudgingly. A snort. *Till we get to the knife-in-the-back part.*

Privately—well, never that—Pen thought that fight would amuse her, too. By her nature, Des *relished* chaos.

He folded his outer garb, donned his nightshirt, and lay down on the creaking cot, pulling up the coarse blanket. "So what's the inventory of bedding vermin tonight, Des?"

"Surprisingly little," she said aloud through his mouth—he shared his tongue freely with her when they were alone, a courtesy she appreciated, though it sometimes alarmed nervous listeners who feared it a sign his demon was ascending. "A few fleas, some head-lice eggs…" A flush of warmth. "Now none, so rest easy, dear Pen." She smacked his lips in a dissatisfied way. "Barely a bedtime snack."

The most efficient way for Des to shed her excess chaos was by killing small, theologically allowed vermin, the fall from life to death being the steepest slope from order to disorder possible. But the lives of a few fleas were hardly sufficient to balance the level of magic they sometimes used.

"You may have any remaining flies in the blacksmith's stable tomorrow morning. And when we get up in the mountains, I can do some hunting for you. Camp dinners, after all. We may need to stretch our rations."

She settled down, pacified with this promise of future slaughter. Pen wriggled into the lumps of the cot's wool-stuffed mattress, and, soon, slept.

ON THE road to Berbak the next morning, Roz studied his future windfall. The golden goose gazed all around, blue eyes bright with curiosity, as if he'd

Penric and the BANDIT

never seen hills or hamlets before. True, he'd not seen these in Oxousa. He murmured to himself under his breath occasionally, his lips twitching in an internal amusement not shared aloud. At least his horsemanship seemed steady.

"You ride well, for a, what, scribe?" Roz began, by way of lure to some revealing talk.

Penric lifted a hand from his reins and wriggled his faintly spotted fingers. "I do a lot of writing in my regular work, yes. But I grew up a country lad, back in the Cantons. My family were...farmers of a sort. Town life came to me later on." He eyed Roz's skinny horse, and the scruffy mule he towed. "And yourself?"

Roz shrugged. "A poor village. My family shared the village garden plots, and did what tasks came their way. Dull place. I was a younger son, so there was no chance of any inheritance for me."

"Ah, I was a younger son, too. Though I'd no desire to inherit my father's land, or life. Did you join the army to escape?"

Roz scoffed. "Even as a youth, I wasn't *that* stupid. I was offered up by my village for the labor conscription." And glad enough they had been to see the back of him, taken away in this annual sacrifice. All right, he and his friends had been wild youngsters, but the dusty village had been so *hopeless*. "The only thing worse than paying a tax is being the payment. I spent the next two years repairing roads for the High Orban of Grabyat. Which would have been more interesting if it hadn't been the same road. My term was about to end when more Rusylli raids came, and the army, in a hurry, conscripted the labor gangs in turn. And we were marched off on the roads we'd built. We weren't best pleased, but camp life was no worse than the road gang. Which isn't saying much." Till they'd come to the actual fighting. That had been a whole new world of worse.

Penric nodded as if in understanding, which seemed unlikely to Roz from such a soft-looking fellow. "One of my older brothers signed up with a mercenary company from Carpagamo, who'd been recruiting men in the Cantons. It seemed a quick way for a younger son to gain a fortune. But it only sped him to a death of a camp fever. I was glad my literacy gave me another way out. Do you read and write?"

"Not well." Or at all. Roz and the dreary old Temple acolyte who doubled as the sometime-

Penric and the BANDIT

schoolteacher for the three villages around had been at odds from the beginning.

"I could teach you a little, if you've a mind," offered Penric. "Would you like to learn?"

"…Not really."

"Mm." Penric left it at that, to Roz's relief.

The road was gradually rising toward the more distant heights. Better watered here, the sparse woods thickened between tiny settlements, their deeper green browning at the edges in the late summer air. Once, they were passed by a merchant's mule train going the other way, packsaddles loaded. By habit, Roz sized it up. It was a longish train, with too many guards and grooms for a small bandit gang to tackle. Always the trade-off; a bigger gang could take more prey, but had to share it around among more mouths, and large caravans were fewer. And the more men in the gang, from more varied origins, the more ugly the infighting grew among them. He'd learned his lesson about that. A gang of one, Roz supposed, was the ultimate simplification. Except it reduced that man to mere *pilfering*, which was no way to capture the fortune that would allow him to *stop*.

Roz thought back over the goose's first remarks. Regular work. Not a scribe, yet a lot of writing. Some town clerk? Secretary to a rich patron? Something that gave him enough funds for his search, yet not enough to leave him untempted to take the risks of his fortune-hunt. Or else the fortune he sought was golden indeed...

As the sun reached its peak, they stopped by a bridge where a stream crossed, to water and rest their mounts and unpack the lunch bought from last night's taverna. Penric paused before eating to bless the meal with a formal prayer, making a tally of the five gods over his torso and murmuring special thanks to the Mother of Summer for the bread, and to the Son of Autumn for the meat. He'd made such a tally before dinner last night, too, Roz recalled. Was he one of those tediously religious people who went on and on about the ever-invisible gods Who had never, as far as Roz could tell, answered a prayer from him? Penric was not inclined to sermonize, at least. Roz wasn't sure what god he ought to thank for that.

Munching, Penric eyed Roz's mule, hobbled to browse along the river margin, with its empty pack-saddle. "You know, it occurs to me, if I find this temple and what I seek in it, it might make more of a load than will fit in my saddlebags. Optimistic, perhaps, but I like to be prepared."

Penric and the BANDIT

"Are you thinking of buying my mule? You might have said so sooner, and saved me a ride to Berbak." Not that Roz had anywhere else to go.

Penric shook his head. "I have no wish to own a mule. Nor did I bring funds to buy livestock." (Roz noted that clue.) "Nor am I certain that I'll really need the added transport. But I wondered if you would be willing to put off selling it for, oh, an extra week, and rent it to me?"

Roz made a doubtful noise, inwardly alert at this new opening, if hardly the one the goose was imagining. Best not appear too eager. "I should not like to risk losing it." Whether through accident or theft he left politely unvoiced. "I'm not against the idea, mind you. But it's my sole purse for the next month, or will be once I turn it into coin. That being by far the best way to eat a mule."

Pen grinned at his joke.

"What say instead…you rent my mule, and I ride along with you till you discover whether you need it or not?"

Pen's brows rose. "That could work well. I don't know if you care to be also hired for a week as a servant…? The beast will need a groom, certainly.

Or have you some other destination, or constraint of time?"

"Not at the moment." Only to outrun the threat of retribution, should his trail of sold mules be followed. Diverting up a random mountain valley would hide him as well, or better, than going to ground in some village. If Roz hadn't expected this side jaunt, it could hardly be anticipated by his possible trackers, either. "I think that could work, too."

Penric nodded cheerfully.

As they mounted up and took the sunlit road southeast once more, Roz thought about destinations. Had he ever had one? All his passions in life so far had been about getting *away*—away from the village, away from the work gang, away from the army. Away from the horrors that had followed after. Had he ever had a *toward*? None to be found in going backward, that was certain. Over the border to Grabyat lay only the threat of execution, or, almost worse to anticipate, becoming a prisoner outright on another work gang, this time with added chains. There could be no returning to his more recent comrades, either, although…if he had enough coin in hand, might he *buy* his way back to forgiveness? It seemed a poor bargain.

Penric and the BANDIT

As the two horses and a mule plodded along, he tried to picture what kind of *toward* a *real* treasure might purchase.

THE LITTLE town of Berbak, Pen judged as he and Roz rode in, must be high enough up in something resembling real mountains to experience something resembling real winters. Instead of the open atriums of houses in mild Orbas and Cedonia, their close gray stone walls were lidded with tile roofs. His eye quickly located the town temple, just off the market square, by its six sides and adjoining courtyard, beside which lay the stable for the sacred animals. The temple's walls and arches were made charming by courses of contrasting cream and rust-colored cut blocks. It looked busy at the moment, a cluster of people milling under the portico. He would come back later, after dinner, when the local divine was more likely to be free of the day's duties.

Berbak actually boasted not one but two inns. Pen chose the cleaner-looking of them, then wondered if he should have picked the other when, instead of taking a room, Roz bargained for a cheaper bed in the inn's stable loft. To better guard their animals, he said, though the innkeeper protested that they would be well looked after by her servants. Pen wondered if Roz was thinking it the better for making off with their mounts in the night, but was not thereby moved to offer to share his own chamber and its expenses. Des would let him know if anything so interesting was occurring.

Roz did yield to the excellent smells from the inn's kitchen, despite the claimed flatness of his purse, and they shared a less cursory meal than last night's. Pen excused himself from another offered game of dice, with perhaps a more interesting stake this time? by voicing a wish to visit the temple to view its interior frescoes and tilework, and pray for luck in their coming quest.

"The luck of the gods has never favored me," Roz said, his mouth twisting up on one side. "Perchance They'll like you better."

Pen was not, at this stage, about to even *attempt* to describe what the attentions of the gods did for him. *Or yours for Them*, reflected Des. He merely smiled and waved himself out into the cooling dusk.

The walk to the square was short, and he was timely; someone wearing the tabard of a dedicat had

Penric and the BANDIT

just come out to close and bar the front doors for the night.

"Well met, sir," he greeted this porter politely. "Is there time for one more prayer tonight? I'm a traveler here, and I wished to take some counsel of your learned divine."

"There is always time for prayer, inside the temple or out," the dedicat returned, assessing him in the dim light of the portico's hanging lantern, and finding no weapons or other obvious threat. "But perhaps there is a little more within, if your matter isn't long."

"It shouldn't be."

The man nodded, a bit provisionally, and admitted him, leading the way across the temple hall. Des's dark-sight relieved the shadows without Pen needing to ask. The place would be dim even in the daytime, its roof lacking an oculus to emit the smoke from the sacred fire on the central plinth; instead it sported a beaten metal hood narrowing to a chimney pipe, reminiscent of the temples of Pen's colder homeland. Altars for each of the five gods took up their accustomed side walls, and Pen made a surreptitious tally sign in Their honors. The back exit was, as common, discreetly sited by the Bastard's altar opposite the front doors, and led into a small rectangular courtyard, almost a light well, with the temple's more utilitarian rooms around. His guide knocked on a door clearly the divine's study, and was bade to enter.

This chamber was better lit, with lamps and wall sconces, hosting familiar clutter: robes on pegs, other gear piled in the corners, rather scanty bookshelves, and a writing table occupied by a man and the day's record-keeping. The man looked up from his scratching quill as his dedicat announced, "Learned Eginah, sir, this traveler says he seeks your counsel."

Which had been the right word by which to gain entry; *counsel* was a religious duty for divines. This was more usually understood as spiritual rather than travel advice, but who knew how one might lead to the other? So the man merely sighed as he laid his interrupted work aside and turned to Pen, fixing a welcoming near-smile on his features. Pen had been hoping for an elderly cleric, who would know this district and his flock from older days, but the fellow was maybe thirty. Unclear how long he'd held this post. Well, all would emerge in due course.

Penric and the BANDIT

"Good evening, Learned." Pen sketched a courteous bow. "I'm a stranger just arrived, on something of a pilgrimage, and I thought you might be the best person to ask for guidance."

The man nodded in resignation, and waved Pen to pull up a stool by the table, and his dedicat back to his duties of securing the temple for the night.

"*Something* of a pilgrimage?" Eginah repeated dubiously after Pen had settled himself and proffered his given name. Though not his surname or status. "Or just a holiday?"

"The root of holiday is *holy day*, so the two are surely compatible, sir. My journey partakes of both."

"The five purposes of pilgrimage, as the five purposes of prayer of which it is a form, are service, supplication, gratitude, divination, and atonement," the divine recited a touch sternly. "Which need is yours?"

Pen thought it over with the seriousness deserved. Gratitude would certainly follow if he were successful. Service…might be in one's point of view. The archdivines of Orbas and of Trigonie, in the latter of which Oxousa was currently a district, could differ from each other sharply on that aspect. Likewise atonement.

Atonement, really? murmured Des. *I thought repentance had to come first. Which you are quite lacking, at the moment.*

I'm thinking of our new friend Roz.

Ha. Good luck on that one.

"All, of them, in part," Pen said, "though I'm hoping you can spare me the need for divination. I seek a fascinating temple, or perhaps school, in this district that I read about in an old book. I wonder if you could help me pinpoint its location. I have a map, but it's short on useful landmarks." Pen unrolled this aid and rose to lay it out before Eginah, who absently used his desk detritus to weigh the corners. "It's called the seminary of Gramez, or sometimes the Hermitage of Aziji."

Eginah pursed his lips and, much like Roz before him, bent to peer. "I've never heard of it."

"I'm guessing it should be in your temple's gift, unless there's some larger town nearby that claims it." Pen gestured off the edge of his map.

"Not really, till over the district border..." Eginah wrinkled his nose and rose. "Stay a moment."

He exited, Des tracking his movement, off to what was possibly the refectory or kitchen at the rear of the building. He came back in a while escorting an elderly, *oh good*, woman servant; cook, by her apron and aroma. She smiled in surprise when Pen rose and offered her a bow equal to the one he'd bestowed on her divine; her smile broadened as she looked him up and down while he introduced himself again, learning her name in turn. He repeated the description of his goal.

She, too, frowned down at his map. "I remember my grandfather talking about this place. He was a carter, and he'd gone out to help some people move from there. He complained mightily about how high and inconvenient it was, and how he'd never go there again."

Bless the old man's ire, then, to have given his granddaughter something striking enough to recall so many decades later. Though Pen spared a moment's concern about what might have been carted out along with the people.

"But the place was abandoned ages ago," she added.

"Oh, no!" said Penric, hoping his shocked tone would entice more details.

The cook shrugged as if in apology, and kindly went on, "The saint was long dead by then. Saint of the Bastard, they said, though what saints of that god do I've never rightly understood."

Good to confirm the eponymous saint had been a fellow devotee of Pen's—his scattered sources had been unclear on that point.

"If it's a seminary you seek, to further your religious education perhaps, I can recommend the one in Trigonie," Eginah offered in compensation. "I graduated from it myself, a few years back."

Pen had been there, more than once, although to impart learning rather than seek it. Luckily for his discretion on this trip, he and Eginah evidently hadn't crossed paths there. "It's more the hermitage of the saint I was interested in. I would still like to visit it, to pay my respects to the departed." Pen tapped the back of his thumb to his lips.

"Have you some special relationship to the fifth god?" asked Eginah, puzzled.

"He has my allegiance, yes." *And I, His, apparently.* Always an ambiguous blessing.

Briefly rising brows from his audience, though no comments; they were obviously trying to guess where to peg him in this broad slot, of all things out of season that fit nowhere else. A bastard (no), a man of odd loves, (no, though he wouldn't vouch

Penric and the BANDIT

for Des's snarled history), criminal or executioner, no, he was too obviously not a workman, though they were perhaps not thinking of embezzlers or other more literate swindlers; comic poet or musician or artist, perhaps. Nobody asked.

Sorcerer remained unsuspected, good. No one he'd encountered yet in Oxousa was touched with second sight, or Des's centuries-deep soul density would have been immediately apparent to them. *That* digression here would have delayed him considerably.

He brought them back to his map where, between them, they were able to rule out a number of wrong turns and blind alleys, with landmarks. For which he was grateful, as he had limited time for this whole—mostly—personal indulgence. Pen snitched the divine's quill to jot notes in the margins.

"Thank you *so much*," he told them sincerely, re-rolling his map and rising to go. And also returning the quill.

"I'll escort you out," said the divine politely, or perhaps prudently. No one wanted to lose small, sellable altar furnishings to light-fingered guests. Eginah, his lamp raised, paused in surprise when Pen actually stopped to pray in the temple hall, and watched with curiosity to see which gods he favored, or more likely wanted favors from.

Since he was praying for the safety of all whom he'd left at home, it was definitely favors-from, tonight. He knelt before each altar in turn, murmuring his beseechings under his breath, words by heart but not rote. The Daughter of Spring for his daughters Rina and Otta. The Mother of Summer for Nikys, who had graduated from Spring's to Summer's cloak upon the birth of their first child, and for Nikys's own mother Idrene. The Son of Autumn for his son Wyn, a god unexpectedly regained for Pen after being abandoned so long ago on a Canton roadside. The Bastard for His own demon Desdemona, and Otta's young demon Atto.

You are the first sorcerer I ever knew of, murmured Des, *to pray for the good of their demon.*

If my teachings prosper, I hope the custom will catch on.

You've left out one, she noted. *Or shall I make the prayer this time?*

If you like. Touched, he knelt before the altar of the Father of Winter, another god lately added to his personal repertoire, and listened while Des repeated

Penric and the BANDIT

his silent prayer for safety. For *him*. He trusted the god was also pleased, if possibly surprised.

Pen rose and made the rounds of the locked offering boxes, dropping a coin in each, and two for the fifth god from him and Des both. Eginah's brows climbed again, and he thanked Pen in turn. Well, it wasn't as if Pen didn't know what kind of gratitude a temple, if not necessarily the gods, most appreciated.

He turned down Eginah's offer of his dedicat to light the way with a lantern, and set off through what was not dark to him for his inn once more.

ROZ STARTLED awake in his bedroll in the stable loft just a moment too late to evade a pair of knees clamping to either side of his head, a big hand holding his jaw shut, and the cold kiss of steel to his throat. Also, as he started to frantically buck, a weight landing across his thighs, with two more capturing each of his flailing arms. Keenly aware of the knife, he stopped struggling.

"*That's* better," rasped the horribly familiar voice above him. "Let's have some light, now."

The faint clink of a dark lantern being uncovered was followed shortly by the weight on his left arm releasing, then yet more illumination as someone off to that side lit the loft lamp hanging from its hook. Sight was no reward as Roz made out his assailants.

He rolled his eyes upward to take in a coarse face he'd never wanted to see again, and down to the leaner figure seated athwart his knees. Masir was the one man he'd regretted abandoning; the sole survivor, besides Roz, of his village work crew, the army, the desperate desertion, the early, awkward thievery, and their worse union with the greater bandit gang. The only man here who wouldn't slit his throat in a heartbeat, without regret. Masir, Roz hoped, would at least be sorry, though any hesitation wasn't likely to make a difference. Tabac, at Roz's head, would murder him with the bored efficiency of a man killing a chicken for dinner.

Lantern-man was turning out Roz's saddlebags. He rattled the thin purse he found, and shook his head at Tabac.

"Where'd you hide the money, thief?" growled Tabac.

"You'll have to let go of his jaw if you want an answer," Masir pointed out.

Penric and the BANDIT

A hard squeeze. "Don't cry out. No one will hear."

"Also," observed Lantern-man, falsely genial, "they'd hang you right along with us."

As the grip released Roz gasped, "What did you do to the night ostler?" A rather aged stable guard; Roz had been talking with him earlier, when being guided to the loft bed. He'd been hospitable, sympathetic to Roz's apparent poverty.

Masir grinned down at him. "We took a trick from you. Garin is getting him drunk and letting him win at dice. He won't pay attention to much till he starts to lose. By which time he'll be sotted."

Not silently slain, then. With so much blood on his own hands, did Roz even have a *right* to be glad of that? But he was.

"We found our horse and mule downstairs," said Masir. "Where's the rest of the string you stole?"

"When something is stolen twice, doesn't it become unstolen?" Roz tried.

Masir smirked, but Tabac was unimpressed by his humor; the knees tightened and the knife returned. Roz swallowed and admitted, "Sold 'em." Obvious enough.

Lantern-man frowned into the purse. "Should be more than this."

"I wasn't in a position to get good bargains. And they weren't good mules. What I got, I ate." Because this lot knew *I gambled it away* was unlikely to be true.

Masir poked his belly. "Then you should be a lot fatter."

Tabac scowled down over Roz as if suspecting him to have swallowed the coins, and was ready to slice him open to recover them. Which he would; Roz had once seen him gut a defiant woman who had gulped down her wedding ring he'd been trying to wrest from her. If Roz hadn't already been plotting his escape from this gang, that would have done it.

"Should skin him for a life lesson, then." The blade wriggled.

"Pretty short lesson," Roz gasped.

"For others."

"Oh."

"Just cut his throat, and let's go," said Lanternman—Roz knew his narrow face, but couldn't recall his name—"We've wasted enough time, and for Bastard-cursed little return."

Roz wondered if the rest of the gang was lurking nearby, hiding in the wooded hills, or if this forage party was just for him, following a long trail.

Penric and the BANDIT

In any case, choking up his second purse, concealed in the loft rafters for the night, seemed unlikely to save him. Once they had the rest of his money in their hands, they'd have no reason to linger, or to take a prisoner who could offer no ransom. The sole reason for abducting him alive at that point would be to make his instructive execution more lingering, or entertaining, in some remote spot where no one could hear him scream. Not an improvement. Bastard's tears, what would draw them off?

"Wait!" Roz gasped as the knees tightened again. Gods, Tabac's crotch stank. "I have something better!"

A dubious pause.

"I'm working a gull."

The pause grew slightly less dubious. Roz had served successfully as a scout before, his unassuming appearance and manners allowing him to gab openly at stops with caravan servants and guards, and sometimes even their merchant masters, and other parties on the roads. Sizing up which ones would repay the hazards, which were too risky, and, a few times, but not too often or someone would notice, persuading his comrades that some feckless group of innocents wasn't worth bothering.

"What kind of gull?" said Masir. "What's he got, that you haven't got it away from him already? Sly scut that you are."

"That's because he hasn't got it yet. He's some outlander lackwit who's come here treasure-hunting. Looking for some old abandoned temple back up in the mountains." Roz did not offer its names.

"What's he think to find there?"

"I'm not sure. He's been very tight-lipped about it. But he wouldn't have come so far for something *small*. For one thing, he wanted to hire my mule to carry it off. I've struck a bargain to ride along as groom. He trusts me."

"Lackwit indeed," muttered Lantern-man.

"I figured for some casting around first—he has a map, but it's bad. And then I'd let him root out his prize for me once we got to the temple. The place has to have been combed over before, so the treasure must be well hidden. Maybe a whole temple treasury! The place housed a saint, it must have been collecting rich offerings for decades!" Would they bite at this inflated bait? Should he elaborate it further? Would they notice that one mule was hardly enough caravan to empty such an imagined vault?

Penric and the BANDIT

The knees relaxed still more. Didn't help the smell.

Roz *absolutely* did not want to share his fresh future chance with this crew, but if it would buy his life, he'd have to sacrifice his golden goose. Well... at least buy time. He suspected his life was forfeit in all versions, sooner or later. But time also bought new rolls of the dice. And sometimes, dice could be weighted.

"Just a few more days," Roz begged. "You fellows have never been patient enough to catch the best payoffs. And this could be huge."

"All lies," judged Lantern-man. Half accurate. Gods, what was his *name*...? "As soon as he gets the chance, he'll scarper again."

More accurate.

"He can't evade the six of us together," said the man who'd been sitting silent on Roz's right arm, which was going numb.

"Likely not," allowed Masir.

Six. Not forty-odd. So, this lot weren't trailing the whole gang after them. He counted, came up one short, then realized the sixth man must have been left somewhere with their horses. Roz didn't think that was going to make any difference for his survival. Not with Tabac on his tail.

"You can't follow too close," warned Roz. "Or strike too soon. If you flush this goose, he'll fly. Let him do the work first."

Tabac emitted a not-disagreeing grunt. Looked around and collected slow nods from the others. And, thanks be, at last stood up. The rest followed, shrugging off their murderous tension. You couldn't call it trust, but they'd all benefitted from Roz's clever reconnaissance before. So, greed, likely. A more reliable motive.

"We'll be watching you," said Lantern-man. "You won't see us."

Roz had no doubt of either assertion.

They filed down the loft ladder. Masir, who'd known Roz longest and best, was last. Roz thought he might speak, some wish or warning or farewell. Not that Roz had wished him well at their prior parting. But he only narrowed his eyes, shook his head, and disappeared into the dark.

Roz sat up with a huff, stretching his arms and legs and finally allowing himself to shake. It took a few minutes for the shudders to pass off.

He thought on the old inn ostler, hopefully sleeping off his bad drink below. And all the other less lucky victims he'd scouted. He'd always hung back during the gang's ambushes and night raids. There was something pointlessly upsetting about killing people he'd actually talked with, even if only for an afternoon. In retrospect, the terrifying Rusylli warriors who had been his first experience with clumsily dealing death seemed not so bad. They'd never stopped to chat or dice with him before trying to spear him. (And then harvest his ears to dry for a memento. Some men had suffered it the other way around, and recovered, earless and odd.)

What was it going to be like after a *week* with his golden goose? Had he really begun dimly imagining not knifing but overpowering the silly young man, stripping him, and leaving him tied up in the woods to somehow survive, but not follow after too soon? *Stupid.* He would have to take extra care not to get too friendly. And most certainly give ground when the others closed in. Maybe he could arrange not to be present. Yes, that would be best.

He sighed and got up to douse the hanging oil lamp. After a moment of staring into the shadows, he just turned it down to a glow before returning to his bedroll. It was a long, grim time before he slept again.

AFTER RETURNING from the temple, Penric sat up for a while in his inn chamber, reviewing his old notes and collating his new ones. He was just yawning and considering putting out the candles when Des borrowed his mouth to murmur, "There's something going on out at the stable. It looks like your trickster is getting visitors."

Pen closed his eyes and followed the widening, and dizzying, sweep of her demonic sight. Walls and floors were translucent gray shadows, but life and souls burned brightly, swirls of colors; inn patrons in nearby rooms sleeping, servants settling down in their beds, small vermin lurking in the dark, pursuing their tiny lives. Across the inn yard, the stable was warm with the big animals: travelers' horses and oxen, his own mount, Roz's horse and mule. The night ostler, whom Pen had vaguely noted on his way back, was talking with a new soul. Four others stood concealed in the shadows of the yard for a few minutes, then quietly slipped inside and followed each other up the ladder to the loft where Roz slept.

"Roz's colleagues, perhaps? Are we about to suffer some night horse-thievery?" Constable work was not Pen's job, but he'd be loth to lose his mount. Apart from the inconvenience, it was borrowed, and

Penric and the BANDIT

he'd promised to bring it back in good condition. He slid his boots back on, grabbing up a dark-colored shirt to shrug over his pale torso. Not much he could do about his hair, which would reflect lantern light like gilt thread.

Bastard's teeth! said Des suddenly. *I don't know who those lads are, but they are* terrifying *your Roz.*

The four new souls were now clustered close around Pen's road companion. Best not delay. After a moment's consideration, he chose to slide out his second-floor window, hang by his hands, and drop to the ground rather than trying to make his way through the sleeping inn, risking creaking boards, doors locked—however briefly—and unwanted encounters. He walked flat-footed around the perimeter of the inn yard through the deepest shadows, listening for an outbreak of violence. At which point he would abandon stealth and run, flinging Des's powers ahead. No such chaotic noises penetrated the damp night air; instead, frozen stillness. Like a hare menaced by a hawk? A wash of panic was still pouring out of that central soul, almost unrecognizable in Roz's distraught dismay.

The ostler and his guest were in the tack room, door closed. Faint voices, maybe a clink of a jug and the click of dice? Those two souls were relatively calm. Yellow lantern light now flowed from the loft. His dark-sight turning the stable to bright grays, Pen slid around a wagon and slipped under the loft near its ladder, out of view of anyone glancing over. The hissed conversation above him rose and fell, the words, in part due to the speakers' thick regional accents, maddeningly just out of distinguishability. Roz's voice was louder, sharpened by fear. Something about a gull? Probably not the sea bird, in this context.

Contraction of 'gullible', I expect, offered Des.

Mumbled negotiation followed; Roz settled slightly. Apparently, no murder with which Pen would be compelled to interfere was immediately forthcoming. Shuffling footsteps echoed on the boards above. Pen hastily secreted himself behind a wheelbarrow and some rakes, and crouched in silence, studying the parade as it climbed down the ladder.

Ordinary souls for the most part, if more tangled than usual. The biggest fellow was decidedly odd, very few colors swirling in him except the red of a dull, low anger, thick and flat like mud stirred with blood.

Ever see anyone like that before, Des?

Penric and the BANDIT

A few times. We swung wide around. It's...not good. You know that easy seminary catch-phrase about 'a soul too rank for even the Bastard to take'?

Aye...?

That's what it looks like alive.

Ah.

Pen studied the group along with Des, committing them to memory. He would recognize them again in the daylight, dark, or around a corner. The reverse would not be true—none of these men possessed even a trace of second sight, or Pen would have already been noticed, and alarm justly taken. Outside the stable, they boosted each other wordlessly over the inn yard wall, with the aid of a rope left hanging. Three of them passed beyond range of Des's soul-sight; one man lingered. In a while, his last comrade emerged from the tack room, and they both retreated over the wall along with the rope, leaving no sign of their midnight visit. The ostler appeared to be dozing, probably drunk.

All right. Five able-bodied thieves, and nothing stolen. I thought it was going to be a raid on the livestock. What do you make of that, Des?

Conclave, presumably. With threats. Planning for later?

Yes? Planning what?

No guess. Probably not for taking up a new vocation as a temple choir, though.

Alas.

In the loft, Roz fretted in his bedroll, his alarm smoothing out slowly like ripples from a thrown stone, reflecting from the shore and doubling back to break each other into new disorder. Whatever that meeting had been about, it hadn't made the man happier.

Pen unfolded from his crouch, slipping through the stable's deep shadows the way he'd come in. He made a more sedate passage back to his chamber, through the door and up the stairs, if still quietly. He donned his nightshirt, the work of Nikys's hands that always felt like her distant embrace when he was away from her.

Lying down in a less lumpy and lively bed than last night's rustic accommodation, he observed to Des, *We may get an indication tomorrow. Will Roz follow them, or will they follow Roz?*

I would quite prefer the first. The implications of the latter are disturbing.

Pen didn't really like either one. If, as seemed a possibility, Roz had been breaking away from his bad company—he'd certainly known them, and as certainly not welcomed them—Pen's plain duty as a divine was to encourage this first shaky step toward repentance and atonement. On the other hand, if adding one bandit to Pen's party had been an unforeseen complication to his quest, adding six was six times worse.

Glad you recognize that, temple-boy, grumped Des. *There's entertainment, and then there's lunacy. I grant you I enjoy the one, but I didn't survive two centuries in this world by rolling around in the other.*

Mn. Well, there's time for the shape of things to emerge. If the roads and trails here are as rough as they look, I'd guess it's an overnight ride to our temple from here.

Which meant tomorrow night's bed would be a blanket on the ground, and, even with Des's uncanny support for his body's health, he wasn't that youth who had roamed the Canton mountains anymore—hunting with and for his demon being a profoundly different task. Pen rolled over to take advantage of the present comfort while he still could.

THE MORNING'S start was delayed by the good inn breakfast, for which Roz had little appetite. His goose stuffed himself cheerfully, which would have been more use had he been a real goose, to be roasted after slaughter and plucking. Instead of his stripped-bare body being rolled into some concealment in the woods, there to find its burial in the bellies of the scavengers—wolves and lynxes and bears roamed the remoter uplands, as well as the more common foxes, vultures, and crows. Pen did purchase road food from the inn's kitchen for the both of them, so it seemed that he was treating his new role as Roz's employer seriously.

The sun was well up before they took to the main route out of Berbak, winding roughly southeast toward the rest of Trigonie. There would be a border marker at the next district, setting a natural limit to how far they could cast for their side road. Roz rode a little behind Pen, with no heart for making more conversation. Though Pen seemed perfectly content to talk to himself, in murmured snatches that Roz could not make out, he realized eventually, because much of it wasn't in Cedonian.

About an hour into the ride, on a rare straight stretch, Roz turned as if to study the rugged

Penric and the BANDIT

mountain scenery behind them. A single rider followed at remove—Masir, he guessed, though it might be Vran, the lantern-holding fellow from last night whose name Roz had finally remembered. They had a similar lean build. No, that was Masir's stubby chestnut horse, right.

The rest would be strung out behind the leader in ones and twos, each keeping the prior just in sight, nothing so memorable as a bunched-up party of half-a-dozen hulking armed men. Roz glimpsing Masir at all was doubtless a deliberate reminder.

The morning and the road passed slowly, sparing their mounts; no courier gallop, this, with fresh relay horses made ready, paid for by army or duke or Temple. Finally, Penric pulled up and pointed to a side road sprouting off to their right.

"I think this is the one."

They'd passed up a few such with a bare glance from Penric, for no reason Roz could see. At least this was on the correct side, assuming the man had been holding his bad map right-side-up all this time, which eliminated half the potential wrong turns at the root.

Roz dismounted and made play with pretending to tighten his girth, and then that of his pack mule, till the first tracking rider appeared over the rise behind them. He then mounted up and called heartily, "Lead on, then!" Pen waved in answer and took the new road, nudging his horse into a faster walk.

The broader valley allowing farm hamlets fell behind as they followed a feeder creek upstream. This valley narrowed, the sides growing steeper and rockier, unfriendly to crops, though they passed a few youngsters herding goats, and later, as the woods thickened, driving pigs to forage for the acorns and beech mast. Pen stopped them for lunch at a little streamside meadow, not too mowed by goats, to let their animals graze. Thus conserving for later use their expensive sacks of grain, also provided by Penric from the inn and carted on the mule.

"Have you ever been here before?" Pen asked Roz as they shared the flatbread and cheese, olives and dried figs.

"No," Roz was able to say honestly. "It's not a traveled road, this." Poor hill families made poor prey, though sometimes, in a pinch, they could be bullied for food stores—or, buying their way out of this threat, for reports on richer neighbors. Or less-poor neighbors, more likely. Sometimes it didn't

Penric and the BANDIT

even take much threat. Envy, like greed, was a reliable motivation.

Roz did not again spy their followers as they rode on, but really, there weren't any side lanes to mistake at this point, just paths winding upward. As the sun dipped below the shouldering hills, Pen called a stop for the night at another narrow meadow, though they might have pushed ahead with good light from the sky for another hour.

Pen, dismounting, just shook his head and smiled as Roz pointed this out.

"I've a mind to do a little hunting in the woods," he said. "I've not had the chance for much of that since I was a boy in my home mountains. You can make camp, and start us a good fire. Set up for a spit." He did delay to help Roz unsaddle and hobble the animals.

Roz couldn't see any objection to letting the young man blunder about in these woods for a while, wearing himself out. He couldn't get too lost—downhill would bring him back to the creek again regardless of how tangled he found himself in the undergrowth and rockfalls. And even if he came back with nothing but his appetite, there was still plenty of packed food from the inn.

It wasn't till Pen had scrambled off happily into the thickets that Roz wondered what weapon he was going to use on his hunt. He bore nothing but a short belt knife, suitable only for cutting bread at meals. No bow, no spear, not even cord for a snare—and snaring was a chancy ploy that required patience, and time that was shortening as the shadows lengthened.

Roz shook his head and applied himself to a fast search of his goose's saddlebags, careful to put everything back the way he found it. Useful camping supplies, including a folding shovel and some substantial coils of rope, occupied one side. No weapons here, either. From the other Roz unearthed a modest stack of well-sewn clothing, with linen underthings and a nightshirt of a fineness, and cleanliness, not usually found in the garb of a hill bandit, along with spare shoes and a pair of blankets. A single purse, not much fatter than the one Roz carried openly—what was Pen *about*, to leave it so unguarded? In case this was a test, Roz put it back unmolested. If Pen was carrying more in reserve, and the easy way he'd been spending so far suggested he was, it must be secreted in a sensible coin belt around his waist. A notebook and

Penric and the BANDIT

a wad of papers were tied up with a string, which Roz didn't bother trying to open as he couldn't read them anyway.

It was all very well-considered and tidy, efficient and impersonal. If the man owned any valuable or beloved mementoes, he'd left them at home. Which was...where? Roz hadn't asked yet. If he ever wanted to know, he realized, he'd better find it out soon.

...He decided he'd really rather not know.

He turned to gathering deadfall, its ready abundance betraying that there were no houses, or more likely huts, of neighbors nearby competing for it. His fire had only just started to burn down to coals, and the lingering light to fade, when Penric walked back out of the woods. He bore a carcass over his shoulder that, when he tossed it down on its own hide he also carried, proved to be a young pig of at least twenty pounds, fully skinned, bled, gutted, and ready for roasting.

"There we go! You can take over from here." He trod off to wash his hands in the stream. Only his hands; there was no blood on his clothes.

Roz dutifully mounted the carcass on sticks and got it started over his fire. This much good meat would take a while, though they could carve off the outer layers as it cooked… At that point he noticed the hide was *also* neatly and completely scraped.

All right. The goose hadn't hunted; he'd encountered some pig herders in the woods and bought the animal, and the butcher's services, from them. Fair enough. Except when Roz flipped the hide over, its fur had the distinctive stripes and spots of a wild boar piglet.

Strange…although delicious, it proved, especially when Penric produced little bags of salt and seasonings from his saddlebags. If the man wanted to pretend he was a skilled hunter, Roz decided, he was not going to gainsay or mock. Not with his mouth full of gift pork, anyway.

PEN SAT up from his bedroll in the deep night—in view of the vagaries of outdoor sleep, he'd lain down in his day clothes. He donned his shoes left ready for this one certainty, and trod over to the meadow's verge to find a discreet spot to piss. Returning, he studied Roz, who had not stirred, with a demon sight that owed nothing to the few clinking red coals from their fading fire, nor to the faint light of

Penric and the BANDIT

the stars from the moonless sky. Taking the opportunity for a reconnoiter, he walked back down the creek-side road in the clinging damp that would later be turning to morning dew.

It wasn't much of a road by this point, more of a dual trackway from old cart and wagon wheels, its weeds cropped only by goats. About a mile along, Des's extended vision found what he...well, probably not *sought*, because that implied a desire for the thing to be found. Not *feared*, either, precisely. Call it *half-expected*.

If it's only half, said Des, *you're not as awake as you think.*

Mn.

The bandit group's campsite lay a little off the road into woods, trading distance from water for concealment. Pen leaned against a tree and crossed his arms, letting his eyes shut more from habit of concentration than need. This pitchy dark concealed bodies, not souls.

Which he counted. Five, huh—the same as last night's inventory. A like number of horses, and one baggage mule, dozed along a rope line strung among the trees, army-fashion.

Look more closely, suggested Des.

Ah, no. Four men from last night, one new added, the prior fifth man subtracted. Who was not to be found straying about in the woods at the farthest reach of Des's senses, either. Peculiar. Possibly even concerning. Although he could think of as many mundane explanations for it as there were bandits.

Des murmured, *Do you agree with me now, that your friend Roz likely sold us to them?*

Yes, though possibly not for pay. Or not only for pay. He was in terror for his life, last night. I should see if I can get Roz talking more tomorrow. He was very quiet today.

Guilt in prospect?

Interesting idea. And a hopeful one? Guilt precedes repentance as repentance precedes atonement.

Eh. Feeling bad about it doesn't count if he colludes to murder you all the same. So much for your tale of treasure. It occurs to me that this bunch is not going to have nearly the same sense of humor about it as you do. They're the sort whose disappointment turns readily to rage. I trust you have a plan for these unwanted hangers-on, Pen.

Several, but which will be more use depends on how the next events play out. The Bastard's thumb is in the surprises, as always.

Penric and the BANDIT

If it comes to a confrontation, don't try to be artistic. And don't even attempt *that finicky narcolepsy trick.*

No, agreed. The older skills are crude, but fast and reliable.

We'd certainly need both, with this crowd. And don't try to be gentle, either. It would be wasted on them. Especially that...odd one.

Even these, we dare not risk killing. For your sake and mine.

And never have I been more sorry for that theological proscription. I suspect, if the Trigonie authorities ever catch up with them, they are all well beyond just losing a hand. Hanging for sure.

A Bastard's divine can't take unto himself the judicial duties of the Father's Order. Pen frowned. *Nor do I wish to.*

Fair enough. A sly grin, not his own, turned his lips up. *As far as the fifth god's kind of justice goes, though, we might get started tonight...*

Till the last moment, I don't want to give up the advantage of our sorcery remaining unsuspected. Nor that of being underestimated. He took possession of the grin. *A little undetectable sabotage, however... A bit of natural bad luck. A gift from our god. As long as we're here.* He added prudently,

We'd better not wake them with it, though. Let sleeping bandits lie.

I have no idea why you'd want them to be well-slept tomorrow, but all right.

Pen walked the two of them closer to the camp, though still a dozen paces off through the black lacings of undergrowth. He began with the obvious, fraying through the horse-lines in two spots to free the bandits' mounts, though the beasts would take a while to discover it. He nixed Des's suggestion of laming some of them, and also forwent the easy opportunity of setting things on fire. He rotted some girths and straps, but not too many, undid stitching here and there. Insect pests were quietly directed to the stored food, and to the bedrolls, and a nearby snake, fortunately or sadly not a viper, was encouraged to find a warm spot within one to curl up. A couple of waterskins sprang leaks.

Ticks were of average abundance here for a late-summer woodland, but they preferred to lie in ambush for their meals, and had such tiny legs... Des did manage to locate a good double-handful of them within her range—happily not actually *held* in his hands—and Pen to relocate them to the bedding full of snoring blood sources. A pint of ticks was a lot of ticks.

Can we put boils on their butts? Des asked hopefully. *That's a very traditional curse.*

From tales, *Des! Also it would take almost as finicky a medical magic as the narcolepsy.*

Wouldn't kill them, though.

Pen frowned, ill-at-ease. His grueling work as a sorcerer-physician had broken his heart, and nearly his mind, all those years ago when he'd practiced back in Martensbridge in the Cantons. Reversing healing would be vastly less costly than creating it, but the thought of doing so with such deliberation made him slightly sick.

Never mind, then, said Des hastily.

He enticed a shrew to crawl into a boot, and stripped it of its life there, as part payment for the increasing warmth of friction this expenditure of magic was creating in his own body. An unlucky lizard, its cold blood making it lesser coin but still useful, found its fate in the folds of a shirt. A couple of dead mice in the food stores completed the night's balancing, apart from the shamanic persuasion he'd needed to position these lesser creatures. For that, he had to lean over and let his nose drip very warm blood for a few moments. Demonic and shamanic magics mixed oddly, and reluctantly, with unlike payments.

I think that may be enough for now. It will slow them down in the morning, at least.

Des, who had been very much enjoying bestowing these boons, grudgingly desisted, with one last mouse corpse dropped in another boot. Pen touched the horses into restive alertness, by which they would shortly stimulate each other into straying. Man-and-demon made their way back to the road and upstream once more.

Pen slid again into his bedroll feeling far too awake. He'd be yawning come dawn. Roz still slumbered, giving no sign of having noticed Pen's absence. Counting over bandits in his mind, it seemed, was not nearly so soporific as counting sheep, not that such a folk remedy had ever worked for him either. Pen tapped his thumb to his lips, whether for apology or prayer he was unsure, and lay staring up at the unfeeling stars.

AFTER A dawn breakfast of all the cold roast pork either of them could hold, they broke their simple camp and

Penric and the BANDIT

saddled up. The goose directed Roz to follow him along the dwindling road upstream once more. Roz tried not to look behind them too often as they rode.

As the sun edged toward noon, Roz studied the steepening cliffs and narrowing valley. The creek was rushing faster as they climbed toward what would surely be its headwaters, and either some difficult pass out over a dip in the ridges, or a fence of stone pinnacles that nothing could surmount. He clicked his skinny horse up alongside Pen's sturdy, and betterfed, beast. It was no speedy courier mount, and Pen's legs were a trifle long for its height, but no question it could go all day. Would they?

"How far up do you mean to explore this trail?" Roz asked, breaking his own resolution to speak less with this feckless, doomed fellow. "Should we turn around and try another?" Not that they would necessarily make it back to the main road. They'd passed any number of deserted spots good for ambush yesterday, where cries would go unheard. But no, the goose was safe till he'd secured his mysterious treasure. As, Roz realized, would be his groom. Maybe he shouldn't press for speed.

"If this is the right valley, it oughtn't be much farther," said Pen, on what evidence Roz didn't see.

As they rounded the next sheer-walled kink in the road, he added, "Oh! I think we're here!"

The ravine opened out on a wide level area before, yes, rising up to a desolate vale capped by ragged rock teeth. Some natural hump in the streambed, helped by human hands placing stones, had dammed the creek into what was more long pool than lake. The area around it, and the lower vale, looked goat-cleared, though there were no flocks browsing now.

As they paused to let their animals put their heads down to drink, Pen turned in his saddle and pointed upward to the left. "I'm guessing that was the original saint's hermitage."

Above a hedge of scrub and trees, a gray stone cliff rose about a hundred feet. Somewhat below its brow, the round, black shadow of a cave entrance was edged by more crumbling human stonework, supporting some porch or walkway. If there were stairs, they weren't visible from here.

"Bastard's snot!" Roz marveled. "How did people get *up* there?"

Penric's grin flashed. "I've seen higher holy refuges. There's one on the island of Limnos that has two thousand penitential steps cut up its rock face above the sea."

Penric and the BANDIT

"What work gang was ever that repentant?"

"I think the penitents are the visitors. I don't know the spiritual state of the workers. It was done a couple of centuries ago. I trust they were compensated somehow."

Roz grimaced. "Or not, more likely."

Pen returned a who-knows? shrug, then pulled his horse's head up and rode over to the edge of the belt of scrub, but the sharper angle evidently concealed more than what the closer vantage revealed. He returned soon, to sit gazing up and down the long cliff. "The cave could well have been supplied by baskets lowered over the edge. Water raised from below here the same way. But unless the seminary consisted of one teacher and two disciples, and I did not get the impression it was that small, there have to be more buildings up out of sight. Limnos is not actually serviced via the absurd steps, but by a sensible donkey road going up the back side. There has to be something like it around here." He gestured onward. "Let's see what we can find by circling from above."

They rode up along the side of the cliff for half a mile, before its dwindling wedge muddled into the rising vale. The fallen rocks and boulders were treacherous, forcing them to dismount and lead their balking animals. At length, threading through the scrub, Pen said, "Ha!"

A trail did indeed cut back here. It might have been roomy enough for carts once, but was now about one goat wide. Branches scratched at their faces, and briars snagged their clothes. After an equal half mile spent retracing their route, a hundred-and-some feet higher, the scrub yielded to piles of rough-cut stones and broken roof tiles, sagging walls, and a small maze of mostly roofless buildings. Many still harbored doorways, their arches and lintels yet upright, doors gone. A couple of rings of stones holding cold ashes told of goatherders camping here, but the buildings, Penric seemed delighted to point out, didn't sport blackened old timbers that would suggest the place had been abandoned due to fire.

Roz put his hands on his hips and stared over the ruins with disfavor. "I don't see any treasures."

"They're not going to be out on tables with gift tags," said Penric, not sharing his pessimism. "Let's camp here. It will take me the rest of the afternoon to look properly through these old buildings. The cave is promising, but it pays to be thorough. Sometimes, you find things you don't expect, that way."

Penric and the BANDIT

Taking the herders' leavings to be as good a local guide as any, they set up their cooking gear by the ring closest to a small outbuilding, still roofed. Pen walked around it eyeing the old tiles suspiciously before pronouncing it safe from night collapse. Trampling and a residue of trash on its dirt floor told of its being used as a dormitory before. Deadfall in the nearest margins of the surrounding woods was scant, picked over, but Roz and Pen between them found enough without too much trouble.

"Are you going to hunt again?" Roz asked. Hunt for goatherders, more likely. Though a roasted young kid or lamb could be tasty.

"I don't need to, yet. Exploration first!"

The first thing Pen explored was the cliff edge. There were no hidden stairs down to the cave or, he said, he'd have tackled it first. A broken-down hand winch did confirm his vision of baskets being lowered and raised, possibly with passengers aboard. They'd have to make do instead with Pen's bare rope. The light would be best early tomorrow morning, he gauged.

Roz, slave to curiosity if not to his supposed employer, picked up the shovel and followed Pen as he wandered through the ruins, a distracted look on his face, humming tunefully. He didn't turn over any rocks, or dig through piles of fallen stone or timber. He did pause in the middle of another abandoned storehouse, its roof open to the sky and wooden floor long rotted in, and pointed downward. "Dig there."

Roz stared at the dirt, seeing nothing. "Why?"

"You might find something you like. You can keep it if you do."

Roz eyed him, from Pen's grin suspecting a jape, but then shrugged and dug. A handspan down, the iron shovel blade hit something that scraped more hollowly than rock. Ceramic? Roz's brows rose, and he dug more vigorously, and carefully. He hoped it wasn't a burial urn.

A clay pot with a lid, yes. His employer finally deigned to get his pale hands dirty, kneeling with Roz and helping him lever the bulbous shape out of the earth.

"It's just an old chamber pot!" Roz said, indignant.

"You have a habit of judging by appearances, don't you? Pretty heavy for a pot of dried shit. Try opening it up."

The weight…was a point. The lid, thoroughly stuck, yielded to neither fingers nor the shovel edge.

Penric and the BANDIT

Peeved, and still suspecting he was being made game of, Roz whanged it hard with the shovel blade till it cracked apart.

The shards fell away around something that might well be a lump of dried waste, until the green corrosion of copper, the black tarnish of silver, and a few tiny glints of gold gave it away. Roz dropped to his knees to scrabble at it. "Coins! But they're all stuck together."

"I might be able to work them apart without damaging them, later on," said Pen. "I have a trick or two. Or you could take the ball as-is to an honest moneychanger, and let him have it, and the trouble, for whatever he thinks it's worth."

"There are no honest moneychangers," said Roz, old aggravations rising to his memory. He stood up and hoisted the ball, trying to judge its considerable weight, and worth. He lugged it back around the broken-down buildings to their chosen firepit, Pen following with an expression of mild curiosity, and set it on his blanket.

They both sat down on either side of the ball and picked at the corroded coins with their fingers, gently working them loose. Roz started sorting his into little piles by metal. He might not be able to read, but he could count. Pen stared more closely at his.

"Huh. These all seem to be old Cedonian Imperial coinage. If we can make out some dates or which emperors' heads are on them as we clean them up, we should be able to figure out when this cache was buried. And possibly why."

"Does it matter?" said Roz.

"Well, it would be interesting to know. I'm no numismatist"—another of Pen's horrible mouthful-words—Roz couldn't guess the meaning or even the language—"but such a coin collector or some historian might pay more than the face value for the rarity."

That part, Roz caught. "Oh." The sort of receiver of stolen goods he usually dealt with wouldn't know much more than Roz, but...these weren't exactly stolen, were they? *Found.* Men didn't have to deal with other thieves for *found.* You didn't have to murder for *found.*

Yet, the grim thought caught up with him, quenching this sudden speculation. Where were Masir and Tabac and the others by now?

At length, their plucking hands reduced the ball back to little metal discs. Pen's pile was cleaner, and bigger, his coins more readable, black tarnish turned to gray on his silver coins, green corrosion to mere worn brown on the copper. Gold, being gold, was uncorrupted, and could be polished back to brightness with a cloth. A good two dozen of the coins were gold. That was…that was a *lot*. Roz blinked as Pen shoved his pile to Roz's side.

"Don't you want any of this? Half, at least?" said Roz, startled.

"It's not the treasure I came looking for. Not expected. Its gift tag, as it were, doesn't have my name on it." Pen's smile flickered, wry.

Bastard's *teeth* what kind of fortune *was* this man expecting here, if he turned up his nose at this? Deciding not to argue, lest the madman think better of his generosity, Roz scraped his coins back into a bundle in his spare shirt, and hid them away again at the bottom of his saddlebags.

Roz stared around at the newly riveting ruins, their ragged shadows lengthening as the sun fell. "Do you think there are any more of these caches buried around in here?"

"No," said Pen. He sounded as certain as when pointing to the dirt the first time. How did he know? Either? "I've one more section to look through, though I don't expect much of it, and then, I suppose, we'd best apply ourselves to dinner. I want to get an early start on that cave tomorrow. I've no idea how large it is, or how long it will take to search." He climbed to his feet with an *oof*, and added under his breath, weirdly, "A few stray vermin wouldn't hurt about now, either, Pen."

Roz, with a glance at his saddlebags, rose and dogged him, shovel at the ready. But a half hour more of clambering around rubble, as far as Roz could tell aimlessly, turned up no more happy surprises, despite a lot of muttering.

Neither well nor spring had been found nearby. While Roz assembled their dinner, Pen rode his unladen horse back around and down to the creek pool, returning with their waterskins full to share with man and beast. The remains of the pork, despite its day's warm ride wrapped up with the feed sacks on the mule, had not yet gone off. That along with some inn food made a substantial meal with little effort, in the ruddy glow of their campfire.

When full dark closed in, Roz rolled up in his blanket under the outbuilding's roof with his saddlebag full of coins tucked between his feet. Just to keep track of it.

Penric and the BANDIT

...EN, 'AKE, Pen, wake up!

Oh, not his confused dreaming—Des was prodding him to consciousness.

Don't move, and keep your eyes closed. We have company.

Pen obeyed the first part, but couldn't help blinking, seeing only the cinder darkness of the old storehouse. *My eyes wouldn't help much.*

Keep your ears open in their place, she said impatiently.

Then came a glimmer of orange light, and the smell of a lantern burning cheap oil. He shut his eyes as instructed, shifting to Des's all-around vision. The now-familiar soul of a bandit—not the murky mud-souled hulk, one of the others—was hovering over Roz, waking him with a hand over his mouth.

"Don't make noise," the man whispered urgently as Roz emitted a muffled choke. Not from being strangled; Roz's alarm was not the pitch of terror of that night in the loft, though his sense of recognition was anything but glad. He must have nodded, for the hand lifted. "Need to talk," the whisper continued. "Come with me."

The man tiptoed back out of the storehouse. Roz, trying to keep quiet, folded aside his blanket and followed barefoot.

After giving a moment for him to clear the doorframe, Pen did the same. Outside, a thin scrape of metal and an increase of the orange glow signaled the man opening his dark lantern wider. Pen ducked back, following them with second sight as the light bobbed and the shadows wavered. They didn't go far, Roz swearing softly as stones bit his feet, trailing after his visitor around their campfire's embers and behind the nearest standing wall.

Pen, with Des's help managing to avoid most of the stones, came up on the wall's other side, careful to keep his head below the top. Sound carried over it adequately; he could hear Roz's anxious breathing as the pair came to a halt. Visible through the gray haze of the wall's unliving matter, their soul-colors hinted at emotions, helping fill in gaps of understanding.

"I thought you'd lost us," said Roz aloud, though the disappointment in his soul suggested, *I'd hoped we'd lost you.* Interesting.

"We thought we had, too," said the visitor, in an aggrieved tone. "The horses got loose in the night and we wasted half the morning finding them. Then Garin's girth broke, and the mule's packsaddle came apart, and we had to stop and deal with both of those. This was all after the fit that knot-pate Fig had about the snake in his bedroll. Before he finished carrying on I wished it *had* been venomous. But I've never seen so many ticks, vile things. Tabac just *bit* them off his skin—even Vran nearly spewed his gorge at that."

"Tabac," said Roz with great certainty—and accuracy, "is crazy."

A not-disagreeing shrug. "Strong, though." The visitor's voice was tinged with approving awe. "So bloody strong. Nobody's going to make a slave out of *him*." A leading pause. "And maybe not of the men who stick by him, either, eh?"

Roz just shook his head. "How did you find us again?"

"We'd about decided we weren't going to, but then Garin scouted ahead and spotted your blond gull collecting water from that pool down there. It took another while for me to figure out how to get up here without crossing the open below the cliff. In the bloody dark."

Surely if they could see us, Des, you could have seen them?

She brushed off the implied reproach. *Not if he was skulking in the brush beyond reach of my soul-sight. I expect this crew is practiced at skulking. Shh, keep listening.*

"Your gull's treasure had better be something spectacular. Do you know what it is, yet?"

A hesitation, a headshake. "He spent the whole afternoon poking around in these ruins, but whatever he's looking for, he hasn't found anything yet."

Aha, said Des. *Roz is testing to figure out if his coin-digging was spied on.*

From the lack of the other's reaction in either body or soul, the answer was evidently no.

They couldn't have seen Roz digging inside that storehouse's walls, noted Pen. *Might have seen, or heard, him fighting with the old chamber pot later.*

Likely not, if they only just saw you fetching the water before dinner.

Ah, true.

"Where is everybody now?" asked Roz.

Good question. Des...?

Outside my range. A sense of irritated embarrassment. *This one seems to have penetrated the woods on his own.*

Penric and the BANDIT

The visitor's voice went plaintive. "Roz, why did you leave the gang? And in such a stupid way?"

Roz's indignation at the trailing poke gave way to moroseness over the first part. "I couldn't stand what we were doing anymore. It was *worse* than the army."

"Nothing could be worse than the army. We'd all be dead by now if we hadn't deserted."

"Instead of three out of us five who fled Grabyat? So far? Four out of five if Tabac gets his way with me."

"The gang was the best thing that could have happened to us, after Ash was killed by that guard. You and me were too few to survive on our own after that. Bastard's teeth, Roz, if you'd just left with the clothes you came in, they'd likely have let you go!"

"And half a horse. We came with half a horse each, I calculate, riding double. I couldn't have taken half a horse anyway."

"I might have persuaded them I donated you the other half for old time's sake—if only it had been the same horse—"

"It had *died*, Masir!"

The visitor—Masir?—ignored this bit of logic and stormed on, "—but then you added the six mules. No *way* they were going to stand for that. You had to know it. If you hadn't gone and stolen those accursed animals you might have got away clean."

"To where? To start over how, with nothing in my purse but lint? I can't go back to Grabyat. I can't stay in Trigonie. To get anywhere else I'd have to cross all of Orbas, and you know how hard they are on bandits after the Red-Eyed General took over their army for Duke Jurgo. We saw what General Arisaydia did to the *Rusylli*, for the Brother's mercy!"

"But Arisaydia's gone back to Cedonia, they say," said Masir, sounding doubtful. "Maybe it's got better, since."

Roz snorted. "And then there's all those Temple sorcerers Jurgo's supposed to have in his pocket. How's a man supposed to fight *that*?"

Oh, sighed Pen, *let me count the many ways...*

Don't give him more or worse ideas than he has already, Pen, said Des, amused.

Roz took a long breath. "What say instead you leave with me, Masir? Together, we might figure how to escape."

"Because deserting with you worked so well the first time? No thanks!" This declaration was soul-sincere, at least.

Penric and the BANDIT

Roz hunched.

A frowning hesitation from Masir. "What did you do with the mule-money, anyway? Because you have to have had it once."

An equal hesitation. "If you came with me, I might tell you."

Trying to buy a companion? mused Pen. *Five gods, that's sad.*

Buy a betrayer, if I read this Masir fellow aright, said Des more tartly. *Sadder still, granted*.

Instead of answering, Masir temporized, "Doesn't matter. We're all held up till your gull finds his treasure. Or doesn't."

"What happens if he doesn't?" said Roz uneasily.

"If they're furious with you for making them chase after those mules, they'll be ten times more furious for making them chase after nothing. At that point, you'd better figure out how to flap your arms and fly, because there's no other way you're getting out of this dead-end valley alive." Masir added as a palpable afterthought, "Your gull, either."

"How long will they wait?"

"No longer than for us to run out of food. How much time is this cave going to take?"

"I don't know how big or complicated it's going to be to explore. It might be a morning, it might be a couple of days."

"Well…we'll be watching. So don't try a night-scarper."

"Right," Roz muttered.

His… Pen hesitated to dub him a *friend*—turned to go. "But, Roz," he added over his shoulder, before he disappeared into the dark, "take your time in that cave."

Roz grimaced, which gave way to a twisted smile as the footsteps faded.

Trying to give Roz a few more days of life? said Pen, considering that odd parting shot.

Or he wants the extra time for something else, said Des. *Or, if he's an especially confused bandit, both.*

The internal debate had to break off for Pen's silent scurry through the shadows to beat Roz's toe-stubbing stumble back to their bedrolls.

BETWEEN ROZ'S own exhaustion, and the dim shade of the windowless, if also door-missing, old storehouse, the sun was well up by the time he awoke. The goose

Penric and the BANDIT

was also still asleep, for perhaps the same reasons. Roz got up quietly and went out for his morning piss, and to check the hobbled horses and mule; they'd not strayed or, hah, been stolen in the night. He walked around the ruins and along the woods' edge for a few minutes, but no comrade—former comrade?—popped out to demand another talk. They had to all be close by now, though. Watching.

When he returned to the storehouse, Pen was emerging, yawning and stretching. "Ah, there you are, good. After breakfast we'll start on the cave."

They divided the last of the roast pork—and just as well to finish it off before it went rank—some drying inn bread rounds, leathery olives, and a few dried plums, washed down with tepid and even more leathery swallows from their flaccid waterskins. Pen undertook to go refill them, and also take the animals down to the poolside meadow to drink and graze on the better forage there while the two men did their exploring above. While he went off on this errand, he set Roz to putting knots in the climbing ropes, with instructions to secure good anchors for them on the cliff above the cave.

Roz took his saddlebags along to the cliff and, upon reflection, also went back for Pen's. The solid tree he found was far enough from the edge that he needed to tie both ropes together to make the distance to the ledge-or-porch in front of the cave mouth. But it gave enough spare length that he was able to lower each set of saddlebags in turn without having them drop with too much of a jar when he released the looping end. He glanced out to check that his horse and mule were hobbled and grazing contentedly below. Pen and his horse were not in sight, but a few minutes later Pen came out of the dappled woods to join him with a plump waterskin over his shoulder. He set it down with an *oof.*

"Should we take the bedrolls down as well?" asked Roz.

"Mn, not unless this cave proves a lot bigger than I've been led to believe," said Pen. "We can decide later."

He tested the rope with a yank, and, with a peculiar grimace, was the first to climb down, swiftly, hand under hand with his boots walking the cliff wall backward. They then collaborated on lowering the waterskin into Pen's arms without any bag-bursting drop. Roz, with an intake of breath as though diving, not climbing, off a cliff, followed. The rock face had some old hand and toe holds

Penric and the BANDIT

chipped in, not visible from above, but so weathered and shallow Roz was glad he didn't need to trust himself to them. The trip down wasn't quite as easy as Pen had made it look, and he wasn't sorry to be caught and lowered carefully at the end much like the waterskin.

He cast one last glance out over the meadow, partly to check the beasts but mostly to check for other company. He saw no movements skulking through the verge. As he watched, Pen's horse, without saddle or bridle, came trotting back on the path down and around from the ruins to join the other animals, head soon down tearing at the grass.

"It's not hobbled," said Roz. "Aren't you afraid it'll run off?"

"Oh, no, it'll be fine," said Pen with his usual vague cheer. His expression grew a lot less vague, almost predatory, as he turned to face the cave mouth and rubbed his hands together. "Now, at last…!"

It was Roz's turn to grin. "Aren't you forgetting something, master not-a-scribe?"

"Hm?"

"We're going to need a light." There had been neither candles, nor a lantern, nor flint-and-steel or other fire-starters among Penric's otherwise well-packed belongings.

"Oh," Pen said, pausing as if taken aback. "You're quite right. We will."

"Fortunately," said Roz smugly, "*I* have candles in my bags."

Well, stubs, anyway. He routinely filched them from any inn where he lodged. Only the wax ones in the summer, as tallow tended to melt in his saddlebags in the heat, but he had a good handful remaining. He laid them out on the cracked slate paving stones, and fashioned a makeshift lantern from his tin drinking cup, with some pebbles to hold the stub upright.

"Very clever," approved Penric.

Roz then bent to work with his own flint and steel; to his pleasure, the wick caught on his first try, not the usual six. He stood, cup in hand, shielding the little flame with his other. "*Now* we're ready."

Penric made a *lead-on* gesture, and followed Roz into the shadowy interior.

Roz did not, once his eyes adjusted from the bright morning outside, actually need the candle in this first chamber. Outer walls built of dry-stacked stone had slumped over the years, creating wide ragged windows. The interior here had been chiseled straight, once; some big flakes of painted plaster still clung in scabby patches. Five niches were carved into one wall. A few startled swallows flew out of a couple, making Roz jump. Roz judged them as altars not by any remnant of decoration, but by Penric solemnly proceeding down the row and making holy signs politely in front of each. How he told one god's place from another's Roz couldn't guess, or maybe it didn't matter by now.

Toward the back of the chamber, three carved-out archways led off: right, left, and center. Pen started with the one on the right. Roz hurried after with their candle.

More painted plaster, less degraded; some broken-down bits of old furniture; and, more disconcerting, the nearly intact skeleton of a wolf or large dog curled up on the floor.

Pen bent to examine it with great interest. "Broken legs," he said after a moment. "It probably fell onto the ledge from above, and crawled in here to die when it couldn't get out. Any creature that doesn't have wings would be in similar straits, I expect. We may find more like this."

Pen walked slowly around the perimeter of the little chamber, but found nothing to engage him aside from the wall paintings. After studying them for a few minutes, he shook his head and led out.

They walked back across the antechamber through the opposite doorway. This chamber nearly matched the other. Dried bat pellets crunched underfoot, and some leavings that suggested owls had been in, but none roosted here now. A more disordered animal skeleton shoved or dragged into one corner might have once been a young sheep, whether wild or strayed from some flock uncertain. Pen again circled the walls examining the paintings, but muttered only, "Very local work," and returned again to the antechamber.

He wheeled and grimaced at the third doorway. "One more last chance," he murmured, and ducked within. Roz followed, growing ever more nervous. If this proved as barren as the other two, the retribution waiting outside was going to be short and ugly.

The chamber was as alarmingly empty as the others except for the back wall, which was blocked with a large pile of rubble. Pen studied it briefly, then said, "Lend me that candle." He held the cup up to the top of the heap, his eyes narrowing as the little

Penric and the BANDIT

flame fluttered. "A draft, good sign. Go fetch that shovel, Roz. We have some digging to do. Actually, just fetch my bags, they have my gloves in."

Roz swallowed, and made his way out into the blinding sunlight of the porch. No sign of anyone above. No sign—he blinked watering eyes—of men or new animals down below. He hoisted Pen's bags to his shoulder, dragging his own back into the antechamber, and paused for his vision to readjust to the shadows again.

At the rock fall, and despite the dark, Penric was already plucking up and tossing aside some of the smaller stones. As Roz plopped down Pen's bags and unearthed and assembled the shovel, Pen nodded and poked in an outer pocket for what proved to be a pair of leather gloves. Thus armed and armored, they both turned to attack the pile together.

As the rubble was not so much reduced as relocated to the other walls, Pen paused and looked up. "I think this is a light-well that caved in. They would have needed better light back here than candles could supply. And air. It should have gone all the way up to the surface, before it filled in with tree roots and leaves and sticks and assorted crud, and solidified."

Roz kept shoveling, wondering if his life was going to depend on this effort. They teamed up to shift or roll some of the heavier rocks. By halfway, it was clear that another chamber lay beyond. Or more than one?

After a few more minutes, Pen held up a hand, and Roz paused for breath. Pen clambered up, folding his body to fit. "Ah," he said, not very informatively.

"Wait!" called Roz. Pen turned his head. Roz scooped up his candle-cup from where it had been set out of the way on one of the larger boulders, and handed it up. "You'll need this."

"Get another out of your bag first. Stick it to a rock. No reason for you to be left in the dark."

Roz did so, lighting the new stub from the first. He jittered as Pen disappeared into the new chamber, and shifted a few more rocks out of the way.

"I think this is it," Pen's voice echoed out. "Come take a look. I'm going to need a hand."

Heart pounding, Roz climbed over the remains of the rubble and ducked inside the new room. It was longer than the others, pushed deeper into the cliff, the wall paintings almost pristine. Roz stumbled over the remains of a big table, half-crushed under the rocks. Pen was at the far end, bent

Penric and the BANDIT

over—were those *chests*? Yes, a pair of them. Visions of gold, jewels, or more likely in this place valuable altar pieces danced in Roz's head.

"Help me get these hauled out to the front chamber," Pen instructed. "Even I am going to need more light for this."

Leather handles on the ends had dried to cracking; they had to each get hands under and lift. The cases were heavy, but...maybe not as densely heavy as that chamber pot? To Roz's frustration Pen insisted on dragging out both chests into the shadowless light of the ragged front windows before opening one.

"Are there any more rooms back there?" Roz wheezed.

"No, that was the last." That weird calm certainty, again.

"Are the chests locked?" Should he fetch the shovel for some more smashing?

Pen passed a hand across the chased metal plate at the front of one. "Not anymore."

He swung up the groaning lid, and emitted a long "Ahhh!" of satisfaction, like a man easing into a hot bath at the end of a long day.

Roz stared down agog.

Then aghast.

"There's...nothing in it but old scrolls and books and papers!"

"And depending on just which old scrolls and books and papers, true treasure. Or maybe it's just old seminary accounting records, if the Bastard is laughing at me today. That's happened before. I won't know till I read them." He plucked out the first scroll and settled down cross-legged as if preparing to do so at once. "With care, mind. Some of these old documents can grow very fragile." He cautiously unrolled it a few inches.

"Are you mad?" screamed Roz. "Open the other one!" His hands scrabbled at the unyielding lock.

Pen twitched up his brows and leaned over to pass his hand across the other lock-plate. Roz jerked up the lid.

"Gently!" Pen chided.

It, too, was full of similar rubbish.

Roz dropped to his knees and clutched his hair. "Oh gods, oh gods! They're going to kill us both!"

"Your bandit friends who have been following us? I believe they may find that harder than either of you think." Penric's voice had gone very dry.

Penric and the BANDIT

Roz stared up into a face unmoved by the terror that gripped him. Not *serene*, exactly, but what this madman found *amusing* in this disaster Roz could not imagine. "You...know?"

"I've known since Berbak. What I don't know, even now, is your place in all this tangle. Well, that you were running away from them has become very clear. I've any number of guesses why. But what I need to know is what you are running toward."

This uncanny echo of his own most private thoughts would have floored Roz if he hadn't been near-gripping the slate pavement already. He hadn't been this close to tears since he was a boy. Which had only got him slapped back then, and were even more useless now. He fought for steadier breath.

"Did you think this was some kind of big laugh on me?" He gestured furiously at the chests of worthless paper. "The joke's on you. You've doomed us both!"

"I disagree," said Penric, in the tone of someone quibbling about an afternoon's sporting score over dinner. "But we can deal with those details in a bit."

Speechless with rage, Roz rose and strode out to the porch to catch his breath and temper. Might he make it up the rope dragging his saddlebags, which he now regretted bringing down, and lose his followers in these mountain woods? This vale might be small on a map, but it was bloody big compared to a man on foot. He turned to tug the rope.

No rope.

What...?

Some noise of dismay must have escaped his open mouth, because a moment later, Vran stuck his face over the edge some twenty feet above.

"Ah, there you are." Vran pitched his voice as low as would still carry down. "How's your gull coming along in there?"

Roz's lagging wits woke up just in time for him to say, "He's still blundering around in the back." The first lie drew the rest more smoothly in its wake, just like chatting with a caravan guard. "We keep finding more rooms, and he takes forever to look around each one. Behind the cut chambers, there's a skinny passage into what looks like a cavern, and the gods alone know how far back that goes."

"Ha. Well, when you find something, we'll lower the rope. If not"—Vran grinned—"not."

"All our food is up at the campsite."

Penric and the BANDIT

"And tasty it was, too. Best not take too long in there, eh?" Vran's narrow face withdrew.

Roz swallowed. And picked up the waterskin to take inside, out of range of an arrow from someone deciding that starvation as a prod would take too long.

Pen, sitting cross-legged by a chest with a book now open in his lap, looked up in placid inquiry.

"You hear all that?" demanded Roz, dropping beside him.

"Oh, yes." Eavesdropping, it seemed, had been a hidden talent of Pen's for some time.

"They took the rope!"

"So I gathered."

"They aren't going to give it back till we produce the treasure. Which doesn't exist. They stole all our food. They'll leave us to starve like that wolf."

"Mm, I have some ox jerky in my saddlebags, but I grant that won't last too long. And the hunting in here is limited. I might snag a few passing birds, but who likes raw birds?"

"Cats," said Roz after a glum moment. "Hawks." He eyed the chests. "I suppose we could cook them over those worthless papers. Those might burn long enough to toast a sparrow."

Pen made a protective jerk toward the chests, and scowled down this not-quite-jest. "Not worthless at all. This volume alone"—he waved it about—"is near priceless. A *complete* copy of On The White God's Bodiless Servants by Learned Mule—that's believed to be a pseudonym, by the way, and scholars have been debating the true authorship for ages—in the original Old Cedonian! With the missing four chapters! I'd only ever seen a bad scribal translation into Adriac, in Lodi."

Roz had only the vaguest notion what or where Lodi even was. Some city across the sea? Or what a soodo-something might be. This was the most excitement Roz had ever seen his hapless companion display. Shouldn't *a gang of brutal men are getting ready to kill us* loom larger, even in his addled brain? "Who would pay for that?" he scoffed.

"The Archdivine of Orbas, for one. The library of the seminary at Dogrita, for another. Me, for a third, though I'll be happy with a scribal copy. A good one, mind you. The Archdivine of Trigonie... isn't going to be offered a bid, though he'll get a scribal copy too, eventually. As a courtesy." Watching Roz's baffled expression, his lips twisted up. "Not

Penric and the BANDIT

the sort of customers for stolen goods your bandit friends usually access?"

Roz shook his head. About to ask, *How much could you get?* he blinked. "Are they stolen? Not... found?"

"Found for now. They will be stolen once they're carried across the border to Orbas, I suppose. From a certain point of view. That of the Archdivine of Trigonie, likely."

"Are *you* a thief?" asked Roz. He'd be stunned, if he believed it for an instant.

"Not in the normal course of things. Usually. Though I did rob some Temple offering boxes, once. In my defense, we were in dire straits at the time. And I sent some money back, later, when I could. Anonymously."

"We're in dire straits *now*."

"It's certainly getting to be a complicated puzzle." Pen set the book carefully aside.

Roz thought of Masir's words. "The only way out of this place is to fly!"

"Sadly, flying is not among my skills, but I have others that might make flying unnecessary. Suppose—just for the sake of argument, mind—I could somehow disable your followers."

Roz snorted. The lanky fellow was fit enough, but he had all the dangerous edge of a wooden spoon. "You couldn't even take down *Fig*."

"We're arguing a hypothetical."

"A what?"

"Just pretending."

"Oh." Roz paused. "Why?"

Pen made an impatient gesture. "Let me try it this way. If you could get out of this place following them, or following me, which would you choose?"

"Neither," said Roz, in a rare moment of honesty. "But not them. Not them ever again."

"Why not?"

Roz found himself launching into a garbled account of all his worst moments with the bandits, which somehow circled back to the Rusylli and their ear-collecting habits, Masir and Ash's most disastrous schemes, and Tabac and that poor gutted woman with her wedding ring, which Tabac had later sold for a pittance. Even Pen, listening with unnatural patience, seemed appalled at that last tale.

"Is this Tabac the leader of the gang, then?" asked Pen.

Penric and the BANDIT

Roz shrugged. "Him and Ulbak between 'em. Ulbak has more brains, but he lost a hand to the executioner for thieving."

"Not too many brains, if that was not a sufficient lesson," observed Pen.

"What else has a man like that got to do?" Roz didn't add aloud, *Or a man like me.* "Tabac and Ulbak each think they're in charge. They've got by so far by not challenging each other. They divide it up, Ulbak for the planning, Tabac for the carrying-out."

"If they did clash, which would win?" asked Penric curiously.

"Tabac," said Roz, without hesitation. "But I bet things would go downhill pretty soon after."

"Huh." Pen chewed his lip. "So, if you were to follow me—"

"Where *are* you going?" Roz had never asked before, because he'd thought Pen's final destination would be a lonely, unmarked grave in the woods. Which it still was, if…less lonely.

"Orbas. It's where I live now. I quite like it. It's much warmer than the Cantons." He blinked amiably. "Have you ever perpetrated a crime in Orbas?"

"I've never even *been* to Orbas."

"An unassailable alibi. So, if I were to take you to Orbas, could you refrain from committing any crime there, ever, afterward? There being little point to rescuing a man from hanging in one country only to condemn him to the same in the next."

"I don't know what else I could do. I don't want to be a slave ever again. The road gang, the army, they were both just slavery under fancier names."

Pen shrugged, not disagreeing. "I've called slavery theft of labor, so you do know what it is to be robbed-from. But between slavery and robbery, there are middle ways. How do you imagine the people you rob get their goods, besides working for them? Looked at that way, working is merely cutting out the middlemen."

"Work's just another kind of slavery," said Roz mulishly.

"Oh, because banditry is such a perpetual holiday? If slavery's the only kind of work you ever knew, I can see why you'd think that way. But I work, at home. I enjoy it. My duties aren't always chosen by me, but doing them well can still be satisfying. Or aggravating, sometimes, but mostly not. And I even get a little leisure to go on holiday myself, which is what brought me"—he looked around, his mouth quirking up—"here." He tapped his lips twice with the back of his thumb. "Or that might have been mischance. Bastard's blessing."

"Slavery and robbery's all I know."

"Then learn something *new*. And then choose it."

"Man like me can't climb out of the pit I've dug myself."

"Someone might throw you a rope."

Roz choked a snort. "Opposite, so far. Who helps a thief?"

"The fifth god, they say. To Whom you should certainly be praying. For a divine in service to the white god, giving good counsel to thieves, and other questionable folks, is a holy duty. Granted divines are supposed to be saving souls, not bodies necessarily, which is a theological fine point that generates a lot of confusion."

"Aye, and where would I find one of *those* in this benighted backwoods, eh?" Roz made a gesture of disgust at Penric's wearing humor.

"They get around. We're sitting in the house of one right now, if I have my history right. A saint, even. Which should be a hint to both of us."

Roz just shook his head. Leaving Penric to roost on his boxes of rubbish like an anxious mother hen, he got up to go poke around the back rooms again, to see if he could find anything at all useful that he might have overlooked.

THAT LAD doesn't pick up clues much, does he? remarked Des as Roz retrieved his cup-lamp and stalked off.

Be fair, he's a little distracted by his disappointment. And his murderous companions. Also, first impressions tend to stick, and I've been cultivating his of me. Pen considered how little he'd known of sorcerers before he'd met one, so memorably, at age nineteen. Magic hadn't been his first explanation for what he'd been seeing either, even with the advantage of far more book-learning than Roz seemed likely to have obtained.

Aye, but all those bandits. Your plan for them, Pen? Our sorcery won't reach through twenty feet of rock.

Unfortunately. He glanced upward at the chamber's chiseled-out ceiling. *For the sort of precision body work I prefer, and you should too, I'll need to get them close. Optimally, one at a time.*

I don't know how well we'll be able to control that. Also, I dislike letting them in knife range.

Penric and the BANDIT

As long as it's not all five at once. I begin to see Adelis's point about armies needing to treat enemies in batches.

Carefully, Pen put his precious volume back in its place, and closed and relocked both chests. "From what we've found in just the top layers," he murmured aloud, "I believe whoever packed these up was preparing to carry away the seminary library's most select treasures. What interrupted the task, I can't guess. Possibly the rockfall. They might have been planning to return with help, but didn't get the chance. But I think we can just load both cases right on to Roz's mule, and inventory them later."

I'm in favor of speed and simplicity, agreed Des. *I'd like for us to get out of here before anything else can go wrong.*

Roz returned, his arms loaded down with lengths of wood from the broken furniture. Pen wasn't sure if he was thinking of using them for firewood, or cudgels. He dumped them down with an angry clatter.

"I've thought through the most efficient way to get out of here," Pen told him.

"How? We're trapped as long as Vran controls that bloody rope."

"Well, you saw those old handholds. I could climb them if I had to."

"To be knocked on the head as soon as you reached the top!"

"That's one disadvantage, to be sure. Then there's the old light well, which might be cleared out with some effort."

"Mine, you mean? Digging over my head while the dirt falls on me? And it's still the same problem at the top."

"I might be more help than you think, but I agree, not a first choice. The point is, we're not as trapped as your friends think, either. But primarily, I want to get my chests out safely."

"They're no friends of mine, and may the Bastard take your rubbishy chests."

Pen grinned. "That's actually the goal. But, more immediately…let's have lunch. It looks to be a busy afternoon, and we'll both do better if we're fed. Also, we need to fill in a little more time, for verisimilitude."

"For *what*?"

"Creating a convincing lie," Pen glossed the scholarly vocabulary. "Your field of expertise, I believe."

Penric and the BANDIT

For a moment, Pen thought Roz was going to try out his makeshift cudgels on Pen's head there and then. But his indignation was diverted to better use chewing on the ox jerky unearthed from Pen's saddlebags, chased with sips of water from the emptied candle cup that they had to share back and forth. Pen's blessing was truncated to a touch of his palm on his heart for Autumn's gift of His creature's meat.

"This"—Roz waved a piece of jerky—"isn't going to last long at this rate." Somewhat in the teeth, so to speak, of the evidence.

Pen managed a lumpy swallow of his own. "It's not going to have to. If you can promise to do exactly as I say, I can promise to get you out of here before nightfall."

Roz snorted. "How? By magic?"

"Yes."

Roz hunched his shoulders. "I'm beginning to hate your stupid japes."

Pen tapped his thumb to his lips. "Also, by lies. The Quadrene heretics call the Bastard the god of lies, and they're not entirely wrong. Trickery in a good-enough cause is theologically allowable, under His cloak. Where I too have found shelter, from time to time." At Roz's peeved look, he filled in, "I *am* a sworn devotee of the white god, if you haven't figured that out by now."

"They're all five the same to me. Useless."

Pen resisted the urge to sermonize. The time for that would come later, when his little congregation was more receptive.

When they'd each gnawed down all the jerky they could stand to chew, and drunk some water—more like leather tea, but such was the disadvantage of waterskins—Pen sat up, clasped his arms around his knees, and began his instructions. Pen could have done with a little more enthusiastic compliance, and less horrified disbelief, but as long as Roz carried them out exactly, the shuffle should result in him, Roz, his cases, and their other possessions up top, and all or most of the bandits down here.

Let us begin.

ROZ DRAGGED one of the chests out onto the cave's porch where it could be viewed from above, and called upward.

"Hey! Vran! Whoever!"

Vran's head popped over the rim. "Find something at last?"

"Yes, a whole stack of chests like this"—Roz pointed to his sample prize—"way back in the cavern. They're really heavy. I'm going to need help carrying them out."

"What about your gull?"

"He got difficult. I had to knife him."

Vran grinned in surprise. "Good for you! About time you found your balls." His face withdrew.

Roz jittered. Their horses and his mule, he noted, were still grazing unmolested down by the stream pool. The crew's mounts had to be somewhere, probably tethered at their campsite up by the old storehouse, if Vran's brag that they'd eaten all their food was true. Roz didn't believe for a moment Pen's airy claim that he would *take care of* Roz's old comrades if he could lure them down here. But at some point in the confusion, he ought to be able to get most of them down.

Then all Roz would have to do was swarm up the rope and pull it up after himself. Unfortunate about abandoning Penric below, but the man practically deserved it for leading Roz into this snare. Getting his newly heavy saddlebags hauled up with him was going to be tricky, but he hoped he could manage somehow. He took the moment to drag them out onto the porch as well, ready next to the chest.

As plans went, it was too fluid and shaky for Roz's tastes, but as long as *Tabac* was among the men trapped, he thought he could still make an escape. Fig he could handle. Masir...probably wouldn't try to kill him. Probably.

At length, Vran made his way down the rope, followed by Masir carefully carrying the dark lantern. Roz waved them into the dimness of the cave's front chamber.

Masir said under his breath to Roz in passing, "If this treasure is all you say, I'll bet you can buy your way back in to, eh, not Tabac's, but maybe Ulbek's good graces with it. As long as it's worth more than six mules, eh?"

Roz, following after, managed a sick smile.

"Shitpit dark," said Vran, peering into the adjoining chambers. "Which way?"

"Straight back. There's two rooms one after the other, then the cavern entry. We had to clear out a rockfall to get to the second room. You'll have to climb over it."

Penric and the BANDIT

Masir nodded and opened the lantern to its widest. Vran waved him ahead.

Roz almost grabbed Masir aside. He was intensely sorry Masir was among the first down. He'd been hoping he'd be last, left on guard above, and Roz could somehow…people *did* sometimes survive head-whacks…

At that point Roz noticed the candle cup and the best cudgel-like chair leg he'd supplied Pen for his ambush were *still lying on the slate pavement.* Pen had claimed that he had excellent night vision, and he'd had more time for his eyes to adapt to the darkness beyond. But there was no way the goose could take out both Vran and Masir with only that stupid bread knife he had stuck in his belt. Or *either.*

A cry of pain, no telling whose, echoed from the back chambers, abruptly cut off. Heart hammering, Roz grabbed up the cudgel and candle cup and soft-footed into the dark, listening for the fight starting, shouts and scuffles. Only dead silence ahead. Was Pen already knifed for real? Would he have to do this *himself*? No one in the first room…the faint orange glow from the dark lantern reflected over the remains of rock fall, not wavering. He scrambled anxiously over the rubble.

The dark lantern sat aside on the floor, illuminating two bodies stretched out face up. Masir lay still. Vran was jerking helplessly, his hands beating the floor, gasping faint enraged noises through his open mouth. *Penric* was upright.

As Roz lurched forward, Pen commanded, "**Stop**." Roz felt as if he'd run headfirst into a wall. With a look of unmoved concentration at odds with the inexplicable scene before them, Penric knelt by Vran, one hand holding his head firmly, the other curling behind his scalp for a brief moment. Vran fell limp and silent.

Grimacing, Penric straightened to a stand. Roz inhaled sharply. Pen's knife—was still in his belt. No blood anywhere. *What?*

Finding he could move again, Roz stepped nearer. Masir was still breathing. Less fortunately, so was Vran. Neither showed any signs of lunging up to fight. Or to otherwise move at all. Which was good, but *why?*

Roz thumped to his knees by Masir, felt for the pulse in his neck, which throbbed steadily under his fingertips despite the flaccid features. He slapped Masir's face lightly, called his name. No reaction. He slapped harder. Nothing. This wasn't the staggered

Penric and the BANDIT

stupor from a blow, but some deeper swoon. He probed around the scalp, the neck, seeking the damage that had done this. No lumps, no gashes, no dying spasms...

"They aren't injured," said Penric, watching this. "Just asleep."

"That's not like any sleep I've ever seen!"

"Narcoleptic, to be exact." At Roz's frustrated gesture, he clarified, "It's a sort of very deep sleep that feels no pain."

That wasn't any help either. Roz squeezed his eyes shut and open, utterly bewildered by this effect without a cause. "What did you *do* to them?"

Penric rolled his shoulders, like a man who'd been sitting too long in a chair, and gave a sharp sniff, rubbing his nose and swallowing. "Do you want the long, accurate answer, or the short, misleading one?"

Roz considered Pen's word-barrages without favor. But Bastard's tears, he was tired of being led around on a leash by this man. Especially when he'd thought *he'd* been doing the leading all this time. Now, there was an unwelcome revelation. Rising, he choked, "Give me the long one."

Pen sighed, drew breath. "First, I knocked them both to the floor by ramming a strong unformed bolus of downhill chaos into their sciatic nerves. This took out their control of their legs. After they'd fallen, I brushed the back of the brain of each with a very much more delicate and directed touch of chaos in a spot that I had previously discovered can render people and animals unconscious. It's an experimental skill I've been developing for sorcerously assisted surgery, so I've had a lot of recent practice, but it's rather important the patient not be moving around as I apply it. They'll be asleep for some time, but I'm never just sure how long. We'd best tie them up to be safe."

What was this blond madman even *talking* about? Sorcerous, *what...*?

Taking in Roz's baffled expression, he added after a moment, kindly, "Unless he or she has second sight, all of this is completely invisible to the outside observer, which makes it hard to explain. If the observer does have the sight, I'm told it's rather impressive, as sorcery goes. For the precision, not the power. Power is wasteful. Precision is elegant."

"What's the short answer?"

"I used magic."

Penric and the BANDIT

Roz tried to decide which version he disliked more. *Both* was true but still unhelpful. "Was that a magic spell, *really*?"

"I prefer the term magic skill. I reserve the term spell for certain Wealdean practices."

"Are you...a hedge sorcerer, then?" Which would explain a *lot*, in rapid retrospect. Roz kept himself from edging away. He'd set up Pen to smash these men's heads in, he'd thought. Why was this ghostly *skill* more disturbing than bloody violence?

...And could he do it to Roz? *Wait*. Had his sudden frozen halt been— *Now* he edged.

"Temple," Penric asserted firmly. "Hedge sorcerers are not so highly trained." In the face of Roz's continuing silence—speechlessness—he added, "Out of the Vilnoc chapterhouse of the Bastard's Order in Orbas."

"Does that make you some kind of templeman, then?"

Pen nodded. "The Order likes for all its sorcerers to be learned divines."

The highest rank, just below archdivines. Roz had never met an archdivine, and only seen regular divines from a distance, usually conducting funerals for the army officers. The dead foot soldiers made do with lesser templemen, acolytes or dedicats. "So... that's why you want to steal all those books...?"

Pen scratched his head in a faintly hangdog fashion. "Book theft is not in the usual line for divines. But as my spare time permits I've been looking for older or lost works on magecraft for a good two decades now. It's a sort of personal quest. My hoped-for prize is to find any kind of knowledge about sorcery that Desdemona and I don't already know."

"Who...?"

"Ah, you have not been introduced, though you've been riding alongside her for days. My demon, Desdemona." His face shifted to a sly, tight irony, alien to his usual looks. In a different Cedonian accent, tinged with the far northern mountains, he added, "Hello there, Roz. My, are you ever a hard-luck sod. Blessed by our god, indeed." Or...was that Pen? At Roz's unnerved stare he went on in his prior cadences, "I let my demon use my mouth to talk, sometimes, that being the only way she can speak to anyone but me. A courtesy and a convenience. Usually." That amused shift again: "Now, Pen, be nice."

Penric—was it Penric?—went on, "You do know that a person becomes a sorcerer by acquiring a demon?"

Penric and the BANDIT

Cautiously, Roz nodded. That was about all he'd heard, apart from dramatic midnight tales that he'd always known were rubbish. Well...that he'd always known till just *now*. Was Pen trying to claim there were *two people* living inside that blond head? Was a demon even a person...?

"Since Desdemona has been in this world for over two hundred, oh, closer to two hundred thirty years, she knows rather a lot about sorcery. Shared with me, to my benefit."

Two decades... Roz peered again at Penric. "How old are *you*?"

"Um, forty-two?"

In the eerie orange glow reflecting up into that too-young face from the dark lantern, Roz felt himself beginning to believe in...anything. Maybe even invisible talking demons? Belatedly, Roz wondered—if the man had been searching for sorcery he didn't already know for twenty years, and by the sound of it not finding much, how much did he know *already*?

"But I can give you a fuller tutorial later," Penric went on. "Our immediate need is for ropes or cords. I've used up mine, but perhaps in your saddlebags...?"

Head swimming, Roz grabbed up the dark lantern and led back out over the rubble to the front room. Cautiously, with a glance up to be sure no one else was watching just now, he ventured out onto the porch to quickly drag in his bags. He cast a worried look at the climbing rope, still at risk of being drawn upward.

Roz did have some cord left from tethering the animals. Pen, hovering, filched it out of his hands and led back to the last room.

"Don't you want the lantern?"

Pen glanced over his shoulder. "Oh, sorry, yes, bring it for yourself. I can see just fine in the dark. Demon-sight."

Penric, it turned out, was also deft at knots. The strong cord quietly parted to useful lengths under his hands without the use of his knife. Everything else Pen had said about his sorcery was just his words, or else effects out of nowhere, and Roz knew the worthlessness of words. This was the first thing he'd truly *seen*.

No. The first thing he'd *noticed*. He was dizzily distracted going over his memory of every interaction he'd had with the man since they'd met, but Pen apparently didn't need much help for this part.

Their victims neatly and securely trussed, they made their way back to the outer chamber.

Roz sank down on the remaining chest. "Now what? Should we try to get up the cliff while we can?"

"Mm, how many more men do you think are up there?"

"Three, if you count Fig. Though Tabac should probably count for two. How do you figure to lure them down here?"

"Curiosity. Which is the same motivation that brought you all along in my train in the first place. Or greed, if you prefer," Pen added at Roz's gesture of protest. "We don't have to do anything. Silence, and more patience than they have, will do the trick."

Dazed, Roz nodded.

PEN MADE a quick last round of the cave's rooms, but there was nothing more of value to him here. He checked over his two trussed victims, still unconscious, to be sure they were breathing without obstruction. He removed their belt knives, a boot knife, and an interesting wrapped wire garrote concealed in the belt of the one named Vran, and took these weapons with him back to the entry chamber.

He sat down with his back to the wall under what he'd deduced to be the Bastard's altar niche, willing to rest for a time, letting the dangerous body heat built up by his magical exertions slowly dissipate. Roz sat down against the opposite wall, warily, as far from him as possible. The bandit—ex-bandit, Pen hoped—didn't offer any more conversation, or questions.

At length, the silence was broken by querulous arguing up at the cliff edge, one rough bass voice cursing like gravel crunching underfoot. Roz flinched at that one; Tabac, then.

A louder voice called down over the edge, "Vran? Masir? Can you hear me?" An unfilled pause. "Roz, you useless clay-pate, are you still down there?"

"Garin," Roz muttered in a less-than-glad identification for Pen's benefit.

A third voice, lighter. "There really is a chest, though, do you see? What d'you suppose is in it?" *Fig*, Roz mouthed.

The chest Roz had dragged out onto the porch for bait, earlier, was still doing its job, good.

Garin's voice: "I've seen army pay chests of about that size. Never got the chance to steal one."

Penric and the BANDIT

Fig again: "Where do you think they all went? Back into that cavern?"

Garin, sourly: "*Lost* in the cavern, more likely." He tried calling names again, louder.

The gravel voice: "Something smells. We'll have to climb down. Garin, you're with me. Fig, keep watch."

The slap of the knotted rope being shaken out was followed by more grunting and swearing as the two men climbed down it to the porch. Pen quietly got up and took position on the front wall where he would not be immediately visible to a man coming through the remains of the doors. Roz took the opposite corner, not quite cowering, his knife held tight in his hand. Des's demon senses unfurled, doubling Pen's vision.

Out on the porch Tabac kicked the chest, roughly, which made Pen wince. "Not heavy enough to be coin." A thump as he tested the lock, which thankfully held.

"Play with that later," said his companion Garin. Pen could discern little about him through the gray haze of the stacked stone wall other than tall, fit, irate, and nervous. *And afflicted with intestinal worms*, Des noted slyly, to which Pen returned, *Which is* not our problem *today*.

Tabac's emotions were the same permanent, level, muddy rage, like a bog of blood. "Aye." He yanked his own big butcher knife out and ready, and strode into the shadows.

Don't fool around with this one, Pen, not even for an instant, Des muttered. *Deal him what you dealt that Rathnattan slaver captain. Twice over, by choice.*

I know.

Coolly, Pen located the complex bundle of nerves in the man's right armpit, and sliced them right through.

The arm holding the knife swung to Tabac's side, stripped of all feeling, as flaccid as a tube of lard. The knife fell from his hand. He didn't even finish swearing in surprise before his left grabbed for the weapon, catching it deftly by the haft, as he wheeled around to locate his enemies, legs bunching.

Taking Des's advice, Pen performed the same ruthless invisible surgery on the left axillary nerve bundle. This time, the big knife clattered to the slates. Tabac wouldn't be gutting any more people with it. Ever.

If the bandit leader could have picked up his knife with his toes, Pen swore he would have tried, but he was wearing hobnailed boots. He still kept

Penric and the BANDIT

coming, swinging toward Penric, freeing one foot for a heavy kick.

Pen dealt a bolus of chaos to the opposite sciatic, temporarily paralyzing it. Overbalanced, the man fell at last, swearing grotesque threats.

Pen spun to see how Roz was dealing with Garin. The two were circling each other in the center of the chamber. Pen dealt three more light chaos strikes in quick succession, both armpits and one sciatic, dropping the fellow to the floor with shocked screams of pain. His knife spun away across the flagstones. Roz darted in and grabbed it, then skipped backward, gasping for breath.

Garin's screams and Tabac's vile bellows were making a cacophony echo around the chamber through which nothing else could be heard. Pen shook his head in irritation, striding forward to bend down, touch each throat, and put paralyzing bolts of disorder through their vocal cords. The noise dropped to open-jawed gasping and huffing.

The friction-like burn of that much strong chaos magic passing through him, that quickly, left Pen hot and sweating, and Des in a highly excited mood, humming with delight like a hard-struck harp string, slow to damp out. He trusted they'd both have time to cool off before they encountered another such challenge.

He stood up to find Roz plastered against the far wall, mouth agape, both knives out, shaking, and pointed toward Pen despite the just-concluded demonstration of how useless they were against a sorcerer.

Pen inquired in a mild tone, "Now, what do you imagine you could do with those that Tabac and Garin couldn't achieve together?"

Slowly, Roz's arms fell. "What did you do to them *this* round?"

"Some directed demonic paralysis. Or in Tabac's case, some directed demonic surgery. The first will wear off in a while. The second won't."

Roz swallowed. "You dropped them in no time at all. That snake Garin. And *Tabac*."

"I don't fight for sport. So I don't fight fair when I'm forced. I prefer fast and final. And going on to less unpleasant things." Pen gazed around. "Let's start with getting out of this cave. I'm done here."

"All right," agreed Roz, in a faint voice.

Together, Pen and Roz dragged the second chest and both sets of saddlebags out onto the porch

Penric and the BANDIT

where they discovered, unsurprisingly, that the rope had again vanished.

Roz, clearly burnt to the end of his wick, screamed upward, "Fig, you stupid dog's pizzle! Throw down the gods-cursed rope! Or I'll beat you bloody when I catch up with you!"

A quick scan with demonic sight. "He's left," Pen informed him. "He can't hear you."

Roz dropped in a heap on the sun-warmed stones, half swearing, half crying.

Pen dragged him upright by one arm. "Come on, help me go collect all the weapons our, ah, visitors were carrying. I already stripped Vran and your friend Masir."

They made a gleaming pile of edged steel in the porch's angling sunlight: half-a-dozen knives, Tabac's big butcher's tool, another garrote.

"What are you going to do with them?" asked Roz uneasily.

"Toss them over the side, I suppose. Those four in there are going to recover and escape eventually. That is, if they all help each other. Tabac won't be climbing anything. They'll have to haul him up like baggage."

"...Would they?"

"Would you?"

"No."

"It will be a mutual test of character, then. Which I don't want to linger to watch. Every man can only offer his own soul to his god, at the end."

"Those knives are worth money, though," observed Roz, recovering himself a little more at this familiar calculation. "Can I keep them?"

"I certainly don't want them."

Or need them, noted Des. *Makes generosity easy, doesn't it?*

Hush.

Roz nodded, and tucked them all away in his saddlebags, except for Tabac's big knife. He stared at it for a few moments, then held it out and dropped it over the porch's low stone wall. Pen watched with him as it bounced and disappeared into the boulders, scree, and scrub eighty feet below.

After a minute Roz asked, even more hesitantly than he'd asked about the little armory, "Can I…go undo Masir's ropes?"

"If you like. Do you think he would have done the same for you?"

"I don't know, anymore." Roz licked his lips, swallowed. "And I don't care. Anymore." He picked

Penric and the BANDIT

up the dark lantern and walked for the last time into the cave.

Without enthusiasm, Pen studied the faint handholds pocking their way twenty feet up the gray rockface. He'd climbed higher with less aid, in his Canton boyhood. But it had been a while. He'd been skinnier. And Des hated heights.

Roz came back, sobered.

"They're still asleep?"

"Yes."

"Good. Let's be gone."

They did what they could with the materials to hand to prepare the baggage for lifting. Taking some deep breaths, Pen positioned himself at the handholds and began to reach upward. His fingertips strained on the too-shallow, poorly angled surfaces. It was easier once he managed the first scant toehold. He moved from hold to hold as quickly as he safely could, because his arms were already starting to quiver. His breath caught at one bad slip, from which he almost didn't recover; Des whimpered. He reached the top and hoisted himself high enough to slide over onto level-ish ground, shaking out his pained hands, and gasped for a minute.

Climbing to his feet, he discovered with relief that Fig had run away too fast to bother taking the rope, still anchored to its tree. Pen wondered what horrors Fig had been picturing from the echoing screams below that had convinced him to pull it up. Pen tossed it back once more. With a few shouted instructions and false starts, Pen managed to hoist both his chests—he insisted they come first—and both sets of saddlebags up over the edge. Roz's were annoyingly heavy, but he was clearly wedded to his little bank. Pen wasn't going to argue about that. It might, after all, be a god-gift.

Pen undid the rope end from the second set of saddlebags and peered back over the edge. Roz stood on the porch, staring up with a sardonic smirk.

He doesn't expect you to throw him down the rope, said Des. *Leaving all the bandits you came with trapped down there. Very efficient. Very logical. Very just.*

Yes, I can tell. Fortunate that we serve the god of chaos, instead.

Formally, Pen made the full tally sign of a learned divine's blessing, properly touching forehead, mouth, navel, groin, and his hand spread over his heart, before lifting it to tap the back of his thumb against his lips twice.

Penric and the BANDIT

Then he grinned and flung the knotted rope out into the bright air.

AS THE rope dangled in front of his nose, Roz thought about his ugly resolution, such a short time ago, to leave Penric—the *Temple sorcerer and learned divine*—to a lethal fate here below. Capping a long, long string of Roz's bad choices. He was fairly sure it wouldn't have gone the way he'd pictured. He got a grip and began to haul himself up the rock face. As he made the top, Penric did not bash him back down, but instead reached out and helped heave him over the brink to safety. Which oughtn't to have taken that much muscle, because never in his life had Roz felt so small.

He rolled over, regained his breath, regained his feet. "Now what?" he asked, hesitantly. It was dawning on him, as relentlessly as rising water, that the most dangerous man in that cave had not been Tabac.

Penric looked around, vaguely. Was it really vague? Or was he seeing things Roz didn't? He poked at their pile of baggage with a toe. "Haul all this back to the campsite, to start. Take stock once we get there. I don't sense your Fig within Des's sight, but he has to be somewhere."

It was no surprise that Penric had them lug his two chests first. At the old outbuilding where they'd left their bedrolls, they found four still-saddled horses and one baggage mule tethered to a rope strung between an old doorframe and a young tree. Roz identified them by their owners: Masir's stubby chestnut, and Vran's and Garin's and Tabac's leggy beasts. Fig's mountain dun was missing, Roz noted aloud.

"Explains why he's out of range," said Pen. "Do you think he's deserting as you did? Abandoning this unsavory life at last?"

A day ago, Roz would have dubbed Pen's hopeful tone foolish. Now, it was disconcerting. Leaving aside whatever demonic thing that casual *out of range* was all about.

"If he'd deserted as I did, he'd have taken the other horses," said Roz. "I suppose he was in a panic."

Roz regathered his scattered wits as they went back for the second load, dumping the saddlebags down next to the chests beside the still-warm fire ring. Penric, too, had evidently been thinking.

Penric and the BANDIT

"I believe we should leave immediately, and try to in get as much distance back to the main road as we can before full dark. The four in the cave should be physically recovered enough by dusk to try to climb out. Or, three of them."

"How?"

Pen shrugged. "Cooperation would do it. Those handholds weren't good, but if I were arranging it, I'd have the best climber stand on the shoulders of whoever's tallest, to cut the strain of getting up in half. Then turn to help the others up after."

Pen hadn't asked him for a boost, Roz noticed. "We took the rope."

Reminded, Pen knelt to stuff the knotted coils back into his saddlebags. "Could still be done. Improvisations with wild grape vines, which I've seen around here, could substitute."

Roz didn't suspect cooperation was how it was likely to go, with that crew, but who knew. "Meanwhile, we should do Fig one better and take these horses. All of them."

Pen's lips tugged up. "In general, I am not in favor of horse theft, but this does seem to call for an exception. Speaking of slowing pursuit."

Roz was relieved Pen didn't try to offer up some Temple-tinged moral objection. Because Roz didn't think he could win an argument with the...not-a-goose. *So not.* Though why did Pen even care about pursuit when he could, it seemed, render it legless again with a twitch of his demonic eyebrow? For that matter, why did he care about the dark? Well, the horses might.

"I do believe I'll borrow this mule, though," said Pen, wandering over to regard the tall, shaggy, flea-bitten beast. "It seems quite sound."

"You might not want that one. It's a kicker. And a biter."

"Oh? We'll have to have a talk about that."

Gracefully dodging a couple of preliminary cow-kicks, Pen went to the animal's side and began removing the camping gear it bore, piling it up for Roz to deal with. He went over the pack-saddle and girth carefully, smirking for no reason Roz could see. He gestured as the mule snaked its head around at him, long yellow teeth bared; it abruptly jerked back, snorting. It made one more attempt to savage him, then stood shaking its head as if trying to dislodge horseflies from its flopping ears. Pen proceeded to firmly bind his chests to the

Penric and the BANDIT

packsaddle, and snugged up the girth—that mule was a blower, too.

Roz gathered up everything left and tied it as best he could to a pair of the other horses for baggage beasts, leaving the two he knew as the better for riding mounts. At a musical humming, he glanced over to see Penric apparently communing with his claimed mule, stroking its face and murmuring in some language Roz did not speak. He wasn't sure about the mule's vocabulary. How many languages *did* Penric command, anyway? The vicious mule nudged him as if seeking scratches, which Penric supplied behind its ears, to its sighing contentment.

When Pen turned back, Roz was startled to see blood on his lips. "Your nose is bleeding!"

"Oh. Yes." Pen rubbed his sleeve over his face in a gesture of unsurprised annoyance. "The price of a shamanic compulsion, which is settled in blood. His own, if the shaman is principled. A Wealdean method. The one form of magic I really would call a spell, and not a demonic skill. Just to make sure I don't lose this mule. It will follow me, now. Won't you, lovie?" He scratched some more, to the mule's loose-lipped bliss. Was that faint patter from *fleas* falling off it?

"What's the price of your demonic magic, then?"

"Death, most efficiently." Penric's mouth twisted in a peculiar smile. "Not the sorcerer's own, normally. Or lesser forms of shed disorder, randomly destructive when not directed. Also heat, but that's more of a side-effect than a price."

Which explained the rain of dying fleas. Roz... didn't ask anything else for a while, after that.

Penric secured his Orban horse's tack and his saddlebags temporarily atop the mule's packsaddle. He watched in mild concern as Roz struggled to get his new string strung, each horse's reins attached by a line to the goods-loaded saddle of the one ahead.

"When I was a boy at Jurald Court—the house where I grew up back in the Cantons—the cook used to say that a boy who tried to grab more biscuits out of the jar than his hand could hold wouldn't be able to extract any. A parable on greed, I believe, though she may have just been protecting her supply of biscuits."

"Waste not, want not," Roz growled back through his teeth, a return shot of remembered motherly chiding that just made Pen snicker.

The sun was riding low over the jagged mountain ridges as they at last mounted up and turned

Penric and the BANDIT

down the goat trail that would lead around to the valley pool, where they would, Roz assumed, collect their other three beasts. Pen rode ahead, his newly docile mule following his horse's swishing tail amiably, without need for a line. Sorcery was beginning to seem a lot like cheating. What in the world could keep sorcerers and their demons from running wild, with all that power? The Temple? Other sorcerers?

Their god...? The thought disturbed Roz in a way that other templemen's droning talk of the gods never had, before.

In the meadow, Pen's Orban horse came to his hand at a whistle, like calling a dog. He proceeded to tack it up with his own gear. Even with them hobbled, Roz had to chase his two beasts down to get them tied at the end of his string, and unhobbled. His skinny nag seemed a little less skinny today, between the good forage and Pen's generous grain rations. The grain sacks were getting light; they might last till the turn back for Berbak, if they went that way. Pen would, presumably, that being the route to Orbas. At that crossroads, Roz realized, he might have another choice.

He was just getting his original mule tied on at the tail of his chain of four-legged future purses when a garbled shout came from the porch of the cave, eighty feet up the gray cliff. Vran's voice—he'd finally escaped his bindings, then, or Masir had undone them. He was pointing back and forth, screaming threats and warnings and curses, so mixed up as to be nearly unintelligible. The fist shaking at them swung out, waving like an army semaphore flag. Roz followed this signpost and, for a moment, lost his breath altogether.

A quarter mile down the valley, filtering in from the wooded road, a large cavalcade of men on horseback emerged. Too far away to make out faces, but Roz didn't need to. Fig's dun mountain pony was trotting next to Ulbak's big bay, prize of a particularly successful caravan raid. Fig was gesturing wildly in the urgency of his tale, or tattle-tale. Swords, bows, spears, glinted among the following men. It was the whole of Ulbak's remaining band, maybe thirty-five armed men, although Roz didn't see the draggle of camp followers; left to make camp behind, or maybe still hidden at the current crumbling hillfort that was their base until the army of Trigonie caught up and evicted them, again.

Pen rode his horse over beside Roz. His face bore a tight, dry smile the like of which Roz had not seen before. "Well," he murmured down to Roz. "This would appear to be a *real* problem."

Roz gulped. "Can't you just...magic them again?" The band was spreading out, like a cavalry troop getting ready to charge.

"For the world's fastest tutorial on the limits of demon magic: no. I can do a dozen things to them, when they get closer"—which they certainly seemed aiming to do—"but I make that upwards of three dozen opponents. All at once. If I try to push too much magic, too fast, through my body, I get heatstroke and pass out. And then you'll have no sorcerer at all."

His urgent blue gaze flicked around the valley. "That said, I would rather have them stringing after us on the downstream side, with the road open in front of us, than to be crowded into some upstream dead end. While they bring in reinforcements. Bastard's teeth, I wish Adelis were here. He'd likely have a cleverer idea for this sort of thing."

"Who?" Roz began striding toward his lead mount. Pen's horse paced alongside.

"Ah, my very military brother-in-law. Who is definitely not going to be sailing in to the rescue this time."

Roz scrambled up on Masir's stubby chestnut, found his stirrups. Felt back to check that his precious saddlebags were still secured behind his cantle. Tugged the line to the first horse in his string. Vran's horse that Pen had ridden down from the ruins was trotting around loose, nervous, but seemed inclined to stick with the herd, or at least strike up a brotherhood with Pen's flea-bitten mule, likewise footloose. It seemed a little late to try to hook it to the others. And maybe futile.

"What in the Bastard's hell are we doing?" Roz said plaintively as Ulbak's army drew nearer. They were all keeping to a jostling walk so far, weirdly threatening.

Pen raised a brief stemming hand. With an inward look, he murmured, "As soon as we're near enough, Des, start on all the girths you can reach. Only try to deal with the weapons that come too close. Snap bowstrings and start fires as opportunity presents. I'll try to deal out as many nerve strikes on the men whacking at us as I can manage."

A wordless *ngh* of assent, from Pen's mouth— but not from Pen?

Turning his head to Roz, Pen said, "My plan, such as it is, is to ride straight down the middle as fast as possible and break through to the other side of their lines. And then keep going, retreating downstream till we can't run any more. You follow. Stay as close to me as you can. I'll try to protect you till…I can't.

"Oh," Pen added after a moment. "I should also mention, a sorcerer is forbidden to kill people with his magic. That's not a Temple rule. The white god enforces it. Instantly, without judicial arguments. Like the punishment for falling over a cliff. It makes this sort of thing extremely tricky."

"He *dies*?"

"No. His demon does." The teeth-bared grin as he pulled his horse's head around held no humor whatsoever. "At which point you would also be without a sorcerer. Though in this situation, I expect I'd be following Des shortly. Sunder it all. I wanted to go *home*."

Pen headed his horse around the long pool and kicked it into a trot. Roz urged his horse after, impeded by the erratic jerking down the lines of his pack train. He'd barely got them all into a lumbering trot when Pen picked up his pace to a canter. No one in the mob ahead made any signs of inviting a parley—good, Roz was glad Pen couldn't fall for that old fatal trick. At Fig's yammering, Ulbak waved his handless arm to alert his men to attack. They began to spread out, preparing to close in around the fleeing duo in a ragged, cavalry-like pincer.

An eager leader closed the gap at a gallop, lowering his spear to take aim at Penric. As he sat back against his cantle to absorb the coming impact, his saddle abruptly turned under him, dumping man, spear, and saddle onto the ground with a clatter, followed by a yelp as his startled horse, jinking, trampled him in its beginning bolt. A concerted roar of attack broke up into scattered swearing as other men's girths likewise betrayed them. A swordsman, riding too close with his blade raised, also overbalanced as his arm fell nerveless to his side and his sword spun away. A shrill yell, and a bushy-bearded man charging in from the other side dropped both his long knife and his reins as his beard and wild hair burst into flames, his hands raised to frantically try to beat them out, his confused horse veering off.

Pen rode in resolute silence. Roz whipped his horse to follow closer in the gap that Pen was creating. A couple of other men, riding frighteningly near with steel raised, also had their sword arms fall

Penric and the BANDIT

nerveless to flop at their sides, and were too shocked and bewildered to even scream.

The men jostling up in the second and third ranks had no idea what uncanny disasters were overtaking their leaders, and kept coming. A man galloping wide around also yelped as the bowstring he was about to release snapped apart and hit his eye. Roz's string of trailing horses were resisting, yanking at his line, dodging in different directions, made wild by the chaos closing around them. A man galloped past with his fancy cloak, stolen from who-knew-what dead fancy woman, fluttering out in trailing flames. Horses were balking, rearing, bolting.

Ahead of Roz, Pen's horse slowed to a trot; even with the backward tugs from his string, Roz overtook him. Pen was leaning forward over his horse's neck, abandoning his reins to support himself with both hands on its withers. As Roz watched in dismay, his hands slipped in streaks of blood, and he fell forward altogether, beginning to list sideways.

Roz shouldered his horse up to that side. Pen's face was running with sweat, as pale as suet when it should have been red with exertion. Blood coated his lips and jaw, spinning off in bright drops, soaking his shirt front. Roz had just time to toss away his string's towline and grab as Pen toppled over. With a heave, he pulled that long body belly-first over his own saddle's pommel. Pen's spooked horse, half bucking, split off.

Roz glanced back in agony as his string lagged behind, soon to fall into the hands of their pursuers. All that hope, lost at the end...

Not quite the end. Ulbak's troop was a tangled snarl of downed riders, screaming men, bolting animals. One last howling spearman charged at them, only for his horse to abruptly stumble and fall. Dead *before* it fell, by the splayed unnatural thumps as it hit the ground and rolled.

No one else rode in pursuit of them, after that.

The entry to the wooded streamside road was not far now. Swearing and crying, Roz clawed Pen's limp body into a more balanced load across his lap, and kicked his horse again into a canter as they passed under the shading limbs.

PEN WAS dizzy, the world dark around him. He was being jolted this way and that. His head pounded. Hooves pounded. Maybe the hooves were pounding

Penric and the BANDIT

on his head—it felt like it. He waved out an arm, caught someone's leg. *Roz.* He, or maybe it was Des, gasped out, "Put us in the river. In the water. In the *water...*" Then the dark closed in again.

He came to his wits a second time to find himself in the stream, the water coursing around him, swishing over the rocks. Someone... Roz, was gripping his arm, holding him, up to his knees in the current where Pen lay. It wasn't as cold as the Canton mountain lake that had preserved him once before, early in his career when he had overdone his magic more out of ignorance than desperation—though there had been desperation then, too—but it was cold enough. The flow carried away his dangerous body heat at a rapid pace, and he swam up to a clearer head at last.

"Good. Good. That's enough," he huffed.

Roz sloshed them both to shore. Pen's wet boots slipped on the rocks, and they staggered out like a couple of sodden drunks. By the time they began to climb the bank, Pen had his feet under himself once more.

The dusk was deepening, but he didn't need Des's dark-sight yet to make out that they were on the streamside road again. The horse Roz had been riding, laced with white lather at the shoulders and loins, was standing still, blowing hard. Pen's own horse seemed to have vanished out from under him somehow when he wasn't looking. Worse, his baggage mule was missing. "How far did we get?"

"Two, three miles?" Roz wheezed.

"Any pursuit?" Des, unasked, cast out her sight; it seemed to Pen her range was much reduced. *I'm recovering too, you know*, she said shortly. *That was a challenge, just now.* The sense of a proud smirk. And a subsiding demonic mania, like a flood tide retreating. Pen could empathize. *We'd best not ever describe this to Adelis*, she continued. *He would get far too excited.* Pen never had been able to convince his brother-in-law the general that sorcerers could not be deployed in military applications. Or...not without destroying the sorcerer.

Considering how freely generals expend their armies, said Des, *I'm not sure how much that weighs with him.*

Roz, stepping apart to listen down the road, shook his head and said, "Not yet."

"Right. Let's...let's keep going." Pen squinted. "We seem to only have one horse."

Roz snorted grimly. "Aye. There's another joke from your god, I guess. On us both, this time. We can ride double for a while more, if I let the poor beast walk."

"All right…"

They heaved themselves up, Pen sitting uncomfortably on the saddlebags behind Roz. The horse huffed objection at the added weight, but seemed too tired to try to buck them off. Pen's clothing was clammy, but drying well enough from the last of his body heat. He'd have to deal with the soaked boots later. They started off at a much slower pace.

"What happened to your string?" Pen thought to ask, after a few muzzy minutes.

Roz was silent for a little. "I could grab it, or I could grab you. I chose you, gods help me."

I imagine One did… Pen wasn't sure when *repentance* had slipped by, but Roz's remarkable tradeoff in that frantic moment seemed a fair atonement to him. Not that he was impartial. And not that he spoke for the gods.

Oh? said Des. *I thought that Temple oath you made means exactly that. Learned divine.*

About to say an inadequate *thank you*, he found it changing on his tongue to a sincere, "Bless you."

Roz gave an odd little flinch. "You're not just mouthing words, when you say that. Are you." The *like all the other templemen I've met* lay implied.

"Not this time. Though if you want words with real weight, you'll have to meet my friend Iroki. Maybe because he has so few."

Pen could not see, but sensed, Roz rolling his eyes. "That'd be a change…who's Iroki?"

"A fisherman…mostly. Lives outside a little village named Pef, upstream from the duke's winter capital of Dogrita. I think you two would get along." Mostly because Blessed Iroki got along with everyone, true. From beggars to lords. As evenhanded as the vast god Whom the saint sometimes channeled. Pen wondered what the long-dead Blessed Aziji had been like. His lost chests of books might have told him…he spared a moment to mourn them. But not as deeply, if briefly, as he would have mourned not getting home to Nikys.

Roz fell silent, perhaps mulling the unvoiced invitation in Pen's words. Pen didn't add, *We could stop and see him on our way back.* He still didn't know which way Roz would jump, when they came to the crossroads.

Or, actually, if they would make it to the crossroads.

Echoing his thought, Roz glanced over his shoulder and said uneasily, "Do you think they'll come after us? They have to be yowling mad by now."

"Um, yes. But also disrupted. Des left about half their saddles damaged on the ground, along with the riders. She managed to start quite a few fires, in clothing and hair. I disarmed maybe a dozen who got too close. That is…disarmed like Tabac. Lost the use of an arm. Permanently. Doing some executioner's job for him, I suppose. I didn't have time to be anything but brutal."

"Did you get Ulbak?"

"Ah…yes, I believe so. His other arm."

Pen imagined a wolf's grin crossing Roz's face. "Good."

"And there was that one poor horse Des killed at the end. I was sorry for it, but she had to dump the chaos overload quickly, or I'd have done much worse than pass out just then. That's going to be puzzling for them."

"I saw it go down. You…did that?" Roz stirred uneasily.

"Yes… I had to do a lot of uncanny animal butchering, in the past. For enough big chaos sinks. There's a whole tale about the high price of a sorcerer-physician's healing magic. Not my favorite story." Pen waved this away. "But Ulbak's little army is also going to have to spend some time getting that crew of theirs out of the cave. I expect comparing their encounters is also going to be confusing. But—what I'm wondering is where they all came from, just then. I don't think Fig would have had time to ride all the way to…wherever, to find them and bring them. They had to have already been on our road."

Roz cleared his throat. "I'm thinking maybe the story about your treasure I told them back in Berbak got exaggerated, in the retelling. Or, um… also in the first telling. I had to get them to back off somehow. Tabac was ready to slit me on the spot."

Pen remembered his uncertain bandit-counting, that night in the woods. "Fig was the man I didn't see in the loft."

"He'd have been left with the horses. He usually is," said Roz. "Not the most reliable fellow in a pinch."

"Adding him back in, there should have been six in the party. But there were only five, that second night. So they must have sent a messenger from Berbak."

"Seems likely."

"Can we expect more, or was that the whole of Ulbak's band?"

"It looked like all of the men. I didn't see the camp followers."

"So we won't get trapped on this road between two bunches of murderous brigands." That was a relief.

"I hope not," sighed Roz.

They both fell into exhausted silence, rocked by the horse's plod. It had been a long time since their meal of ox jerky and leather water back in the cave. Any food supplies Tabac and his crew hadn't eaten were scattered with Roz's lost string. Pen had these steep woods for a larder, along with the stream, and night was no bar to him. But hunting or fishing even by sorcerous means, plus the necessary cooking, would still take time. Better to trade his growling stomach for more miles, at least till this horse rebelled.

With a sharp intake of breath, the sagging Roz sat up and turned his head. "I hear hoofbeats behind us."

Des...?

Stand down. You'll like the load these beasts carry.

"Hold up," Pen told Roz.

"What?" He seemed about to try to whip his stiff-legged mount into, eh, probably not a gallop, but some faster motion.

Pen slid down to his feet, grinning into the suddenly bright gray shadows of the road behind them. Out of them trotted two colorful, familiar life-shapes. Looming from the non-dark, his Orban horse had lost its bridle—probably yanked off by stepping on trailing reins—but still bore Pen's saddle and saddlebags. The big gray mule followed. They made whuffling noises of greeting to him. And, oh, blessing unlooked-for! His chests were still tightly affixed to the packsaddle. Pen welcomed the two animals with glad cries, pets, and praise. He also fondly patted the chests.

Roz, staring down agape, closed his mouth. Then opened it to say plaintively, "Is there any chance my string will show up, too?"

Pen cleared his throat in embarrassment. "I'm afraid it's unlikely. I didn't think to plant a shamanic geas in any of your beasts. Sorry...?"

Penric and the BANDIT

Roz, very gently, pounded his own forehead with his fist. "Magic," he muttered. He made it sound like a curse.

"You still have your coins," Pen pointed out, in an effort to cheer him up. "And I owe you for a mule."

"I owe you for my life. I'll throw in the sodding mule." With some undervoiced addendum about ...*stole it in the first place.*

"I really think we're square on rescues. But when we get back—when I get back to Orbas, I can certainly access the funds to make one mule up to you. One way or another."

"Whatever," breathed Roz, slumping in surrender. Burnt to the end of his wick, aye. And not alone in that, Pen conceded as he heaved himself back into his saddle with the grace of a sack of rocks.

His bridleless horse only took a little more attention to control, it was so enspelled by a week in his company. With the load reduced on Roz's horse, they were able to push on a couple more slow miles in the dark, before finding a hiding spot far enough into the woods to conceal them for the rest of the night. Food would have to wait till morning; fatigue made a fair substitute. Blankets on the ground seemed like featherbeds at this point. Pen did make sure they would suffer no ticks.

ROZ WOKE with a groan when the growing light from the sky filtered through the branches. Pen was up already, rummaging in his saddlebags, drawing out cleaner clothes and, of all things, a bar of fine white soap. True, the clothes he'd lain down in were filthy, his shirt stained brown with that flood of blood, more spread around than cleaned by his soak last night. Two days of beard stubble glittered on his jaw like scattered gold-shavings. His escaping, tangled pale hair, caught with sticks and dried leaves, gave him a lunatic look.

"Oh, good, you're awake," he said as Roz sat up. "Go ahead and build a small fire, as smokeless as you can make it, and I'll fetch us some fish from the river for breakfast. That will be quickest and closest." He stared around absently. "Unless you want roast fox, but no."

He gathered up the stack of clothes and the soap, and marched off through the trees.

Penric and the BANDIT

He was back in half an hour as Roz, his fatigued hands shaky, was struggling with his flint and steel to get his tinder alight.

"Oh, sorry, I can do that for you," Pen said cheerfully, and pointed. Roz jerked back as his little tent of dry sticks and deadfall burst into flame.

Pen was now completely bathed, his washed hair loose and drying down his back, somehow smoothly shaved though he'd borne no razor, dressed and in dry shoes as if stepping out of an inn chamber. He swung yesterday's shirt like a market basket, and dumped it down to reveal four fat mountain trout, gutted and cleaned.

"I'll take care of grilling these. You can borrow my soap."

"What for?"

"A bath, Roz."

"No point if I'm just crawling back into the same filthy clothes."

"You can wash them as well, while you're about it." He overrode Roz's starting complaint of *I'm not a camp follower!* with "We're going to begin meeting local people on the road, soon. Better for their reactions to us if we don't look, and stink, like we just lost a fight with forty bandits."

No, we just won *a fight with forty bandits.* Or... Penric had. Penric and his *demon*. Roz should stop overlooking the invisible demon. He suppressed a shudder.

"Des likes me to be tidy," Pen went on. "She shares my body, after all. Feels what I feel. Smells what I smell." A short smile, and a dry look Roz's way. "Perforce, we live together always, and who wants to be stuck with a slovenly chamber mate?"

"I never had a chamber," said Roz, grouchily. "Or a chamber mate. Just army barracks and road-crew tents. And the guardhouse, couple of times. Your lady demon wouldn't have wanted to smell *those* chamber mates, I guarantee it."

"Just so," said Pen. He pressed the soap into Roz's unwilling hand. "Don't make me use the weirding voice on you again. Go wash up."

"What would happen if you used the, the whatever voice on me?" Roz asked in suspicion.

"Well, *I* would get a nosebleed, and *you* would get the most thorough scrubbing of your life. Self-inflicted."

Wait...*again*? And, *Oh*. Aye. His stricken halt in the cave at Pen's sharp word. So, that skill-or-spell had a name? Roz thought he might start just dubbing it all *sodding magic*.

They stared each other down. Roz lost.

The creek was ass-freezing cold. But the grilled trout, when he returned, was delicious.

Though Pen had declined to offer his demon as a laundress, he did do something to speedily dry Roz's shirt, trousers, and ragged socks hung over a branch while they ate. Roz's messy, but clean, black curls were left to dry on their own, which they did soon enough. So did Pen's hair, which he rebraided into its accustomed thick blond queue. Pen also broke down and, with the put-upon air of a mother wiping snot from her child's nose—Roz sensed Des—ran a damp cloth over Roz's chin that somehow removed his beard stubble, more neatly than any barber Roz had ever, occasionally, been able to afford. Saddled up and on the road again, Roz had to admit, only to himself, that he felt more comfortable than he had in months.

Pen claimed that his demon's sight would allow them to get off the road and into concealment in time if pursuit came up from behind, or if any had passed them in the night and was doubling back. As the woods thinned and the valley opened out into little farm fields and their hamlets, there seemed less concealment to be had, but there were also now people out at work. Though if the gang—the remains of the gang—were enraged enough, the presence of potential witnesses would be no protection.

They approached the crossroads of the main route to Berbak as the sun climbed to noon. Roz's breath drew sharply in at the sight of a large company of Trigonie foot soldiers, taking a break on the roadside while their dismounted officers debated over a map. The officers paused to stare in speculation as Pen, Roz, and the baggage mule approached.

"You're my groom," said Pen in a low voice to Roz. "Let me do the talking."

He *wanted* to whip the stubby chestnut into a gallop and start *running*. But hiding behind Penric seemed the next best thing. *No...better.* He fell back next to the mule and tried to look servile. Tidy and servile, befitting his neat employer.

An officer stepped forward with a polite salute, and with an equally polite nod Penric paused his horse.

"Good day, sir," the officer began. "We've received word of a large and dangerous group of hill bandits operating in this area. These roads may

Penric and the BANDIT

not be especially safe to travel just now. Your best choice would probably be to lodge at the town of Berbak"—he pointed down the road—"until we've captured them. Have you seen any signs of armed men on the road? They'd be traveling broken up into small groups, in daylight."

Pen blinked amiably. "We haven't seen any such this morning," he said in truth. "But I understand there's an old abandoned temple up at the head of this valley"—he waved back the way they'd come—"that would make an ideal bivouac for men wanting to avoid being seen. It's a fair march back, but there's good water all the way for your men and animals. It might repay some scouting."

The officer rubbed his lips in thought, taking this in. "Thank you, sir," he said at last, and waved Pen on toward the presumed safety of Berbak. He did turn his head in belated curiosity as he finally noticed the absence of a bridle on Pen's horse, making Roz cringe, but they rode away before he could remark on it. As they cleared the end of the column with its baggage carts, the officers shouted their men to their feet. When Roz looked back over his shoulder, the head of the column was just turning onto their valley road.

"You know," said Pen meditatively after they had ridden for a few minutes, "it was likely just as well that you weren't trailing a train of half-a-dozen obviously stolen horses and their gear. I expect there would have been a lot more uncomfortable questions asked. Bastard's luck, that—maddeningly ambiguous as usual." He tapped the back of his thumb to his lips.

Roz wondered if that was a gesture—or was it a prayer?—that he should consider taking up. He glanced back at Pen's entirely non-obviously stolen chests, rocking along on the equally demure single mule's packsaddle. "Aye," he breathed after a minute. "Likely so."

Distracted by the soldiery, Roz realized that he'd followed after Pen unthinkingly at the crossroads. Well, so, he'd have another chance to choose at Berbak.

THEY ARRIVED back at the pleasant mountain town of Berbak in the midafternoon. Pen considered just stopping for the night, but the thought of the border of Orbas, and beyond it, home, was drawing him hard now. Instead he called for a meal break

Penric and the BANDIT

for both men and animals, buying the beasts a thorough grooming, fodder, and a rest in the shade of the stable while he and Roz acquired the same in the good inn. He did need to duck into an unoccupied stall and fish out the thin linen coin belt from around his waist next to his skin.

"I thought you might be hiding something like that," said Roz, leaning on the stall door and observing closely, as he tended to do whenever there was money involved.

"I'd hoped not to have to tap my reserves, this trip. But your frie—former friends made off with my purse at some point when they had possession of my bedroll. Fortunately, they overlooked my notebook. If they'd thought to look through it, they'd have discovered my name and rank, and powers, prematurely."

"I overlooked it too," Roz admitted. "But I can't read, so it wouldn't have done me any good."

Pen's lips twitched up. "Ready to change that, yet?"

"Learn how, you mean? Isn't it too late for me?"

"No." Pen did not expand, leaving Roz to digest that.

The meal at the inn was prompt, if simple, the serving girl apologizing that the night's roast wasn't ready yet, and didn't they want to stay, sirs? Pen did appease her with an order for a two-day supply of road food to eat as they traveled on. While they awaited her return, Roz drew out his dice and desultorily began to play, one hand against the other.

He glanced up at Pen, studying this. "Did you know my dice were weighted, that first night?"

"Yes. Or, Des did."

"Then why did you play?"

"In general, people who know I'm a sorcerer won't play games of chance with me. So I don't often get the opportunity, though I enjoy them. Opponents sometimes think I'm cheating even when I lose, which seems unfair."

"Is that why you only play for olive pits?"

"I have a frugal wife." Pen couldn't help smiling softly. "I figure my money is as much hers as mine, so I try to treat it as she would. Unless something seems especially worth the gamble."

"What would you think worth gambling for?"

"Hm. Souls, probably."

"What would you bet against *that* stake?" said Roz, nonplussed.

"Yesterday, my life." Pen's brows flicked up at his confused grunt. "We both won, I note. Reminds me of the great gamble of marriage, that way. Either you both win, or you both lose. There is no way that one winning and the other losing could come out well, in the end."

Roz sat back, fingering his dice. "I can't imagine a fellow like me ever marrying."

"As a bandit, probably not. You'd have to become...a fellow not like you. Future Roz."

Roz regarded him suspiciously. "Are you *sermonizing* at me?"

"Mm, a little bit?" Pen held up his thumb and finger a scant distance apart. "It *is* my profession. One of them."

"How many professions do you *have*?"

"I'm not sure..." Surreptitiously, Pen counted on his fingers. "Sorcerer, divine, translator, physician—very much retired, thank you—scholar, writer, teacher. And whatever other odd jobs the duke, the archdivine, my chapter head, or the white god drop on me. Rescuer of orphans sometimes, if I'm lucky." He decided not to mention *scourge of pirates*. And now, apparently, also of bandits. "Husband, father, son-in-law... A man doesn't have to stay only with whatever choice he first falls into, or only with one. Or with a bad one. Eh?"

Their food arrived then, relieving Roz of any need to respond to this bait. The comfortable quiet of chewing ruled for a time.

Pen mused to Des, *But one soul out of forty does not seem like great winnings, in this play. I should have done better...*

Give over, Pen. If it had been thirty-nine out of forty you would still be fretting over the lost one. Which, if it were that Tabac, would be particularly thick-headed of you. In the last analysis, Roz began to save himself the night he first deserted that vile bandit gang. You just helped.

Keeping me humble, Des?

You hardly need my aid for that. But if you are still disappointed in your winnings by the time we get to Pef, talk to Iroki.

Counseling the counselor? He could be the man for it, true.

I was more thinking he might consult his Holy Friend on your behalf.

Ah. There was a consoling thought. Not alone, indeed.

Pen was just clearing his plate when Learned Eginah, entering the inn's common room, recognized him and angled over to their table. The

Penric and the BANDIT

local divine cast them a hasty five-fold tally as he came up.

"Master Penric! And, um..."

"My traveling companion, Roz," Pen supplied smoothly. Eginah ducked his head politely at this addition.

"Did you ever find the temple you were looking for?"

"Yes, it was up that valley, quite far, and thank you—and your cook—again for helping me figure out which one. Sadly, when we arrived we found it to be all in ruins, though interesting in their way. It still proved an occasion for prayer."

Roz managed not to choke.

Eginah nodded, his expectations confirmed. "I'd been extremely worried about you," he went on. "A company of the duke's army bivouacked here last night. They're searching for a hideous gang of mountain brigands who have been terrorizing Oxousa for oh, almost three years now. They say some have been sighted in the vicinity. The roads will not be safe till the army apprehends them."

Roz was doing a very good job of looking only concerned, and not panicked. Pen cast him a supportive nod. "Yes, we passed the soldiers on the road this morning. That's what they said. They looked to be a fit bunch, well equipped. I imagine they have a good chance of it."

"Let us all pray so," said Eginah earnestly.

After exchanging a few more platitudes, and some well-meant advice for Pen to linger in the relative safety of Berbak for a few days, Eginah proceeded on his interrupted errand.

"I wonder what's going to happen when the army catches up to the gang?" Pen mused. "I suppose it depends on where and when. It will take those foot soldiers two days to march all the way up to the temple, but they might meet your lot sooner coming back along the stream."

"Can we not call them *mine*?" said Roz plaintively. "They stopped being mine when I left in the night with those bloody stupid mules."

Pen paused, nodded. "Fair. And true." He cast Roz a fifth god's approving salute with his thumb-tap. "Ulbak's lot, I suppose. Or are—were—they more Tabac's?"

"Ulbak's will do. Only Tabac would have argued about that, and…I think he's lost his say."

"In any case. Could they win against an army troop? They seemed evenly matched for numbers. Or, um, they were. Before."

Roz shook his head. "They never go on the attack unless they have overwhelming odds. Like they...thought they had yesterday. They'll scatter, and make the army chase them down piecemeal. The survivors'll regroup later."

Pen wondered if Roz hoped his old friend Masir would be among that number. His only old friend, it seemed, with the dubious exception of Fig. His last fellow villager had survived as much misfortune as Roz had, so far, so perhaps there was a chance.

"Unless the army comes on them by surprise," Roz went on. "Which might happen, if they try to return down the road. Only road, for the most of it."

The army would be less surprised than the bandits, in that version, Pen reflected. "In any case, I'd like to be over the border of Orbas before any of them get back with more questions. Or come looking for me. Or before anything else goes wrong. I expect a day's lead, but I shouldn't like to count on it."

Roz said sourly, "I don't know that anyone will be looking for you. Or would recognize you from the descriptions if they saw you. By the time word gets back here, we'll have turned into twenty sorcerers, a troop of rogues in leather, and lightning from a clear sky."

Pen grinned wryly. Des interpolated, falsely demure: "We do our best."

"That was my demon," Pen excused this.

Roz shook his head. "D'you know, I'm actually starting to tell you apart?" He rose first.

If they pushed on till dark, Pen calculated, following him out, they could reach Orbas sometime late tomorrow. He was more than ready for his simple holiday jaunt to conclude.

THEY MANAGED three more hours of riding before the late summer dusk began to rise in the valleys, their ramparts dwindling here to rough sunset-gilded hills. Roz gulped in worry when Pen chose to turn off at a rural caravan rest, a roadside field and woodlot that some Oxousan farmer rented out to such travelers and their beasts. It was already occupied by a large train. Was it possible that some surviving guard or merchant might recognize him from a previous encounter? Roz hung back with their beasts, playing devoted groom for all he was worth, while Pen went off to chirpily exchange gossip with the camped crew. He was gone a long time.

Penric and the BANDIT

"The caravan men tell of no troubles encountered between here and the border worse than a balky mule and a lost shoe," he reported back. "I thought I might buy some Oxousan souvenir from them, but their goods were coming from Orbas, which would make it rather pointless. They didn't bear any bad news from at least as far back as Dogrita. Their report chain doesn't seem to extend to the coast."

Where Penric's home city of Vilnoc lay, on a sea Roz had never seen. Nor had he ever glimpsed any other sea, come to think. He wondered how different the sight might feel compared to inland lakes.

"What would a man like me ever find to do in a big port city?" Roz said slowly. "I've never been to such a place. Even at the country towns we camped beside when I was in the army, I never had to decide anything for myself. When we were let off to look around, I always went with some fellows, who did the picking."

Penric shrugged, sitting there all golden from the flickering light of their little campfire, which he'd lit, as far as Roz could tell, with nothing but a distant finger-flick...and the hidden demon. "There are hundreds, maybe thousands, of different tasks to do in Vilnoc, from duke to dockhand. You'd be spoiled for choices. Well, not duke I suppose. That's a draining job, by the way, I wouldn't recommend it. But I thought I would take you to my own Order's chapterhouse, at first. It's very well run by Learned Sioann, who as a divine of the white god bears exactly the same obligation to look out for those who fit nowhere else as I do. Such as, oh, a refugee reforming thief, for a random example. And she's used to taking in my odd strays. You would be far from the first I gifted to her."

"I don't think I have any religious calling."

"Not required. Though if you change your mind later, becoming a lay dedicat isn't at all onerous."

"Isn't what?"

"Isn't a great burden," Pen supplied smoothly. It occurred to Roz that not once had Pen mocked him for his ignorance; he just handed over the missing bit and went on. It made the asking unexpectedly easier and easier. "But the point about Sioann is that she's *very good* at finding well-matched tasks for idle folks to do. Up to and including me, sometimes."

Roz tried to decide if this was a promise or a threat. "The women back in my home village were all dead-set on matching me with chores. I hadn't much liked it." Though compared with the terrible tasks given him by the men who'd marched him away, and after...hm.

"I felt the same way, as a boy." Pen's lips curled up at some unshared memory. "What I discovered as a man was that it made a world of difference when I could choose for myself what food I put on my plate. Even though I still had to eat. So to speak." He stared off into the dark toward what Roz imagined was the way to his seacoast city. "Family to feed too, now. Obstreperous as they can sometimes get, I wouldn't trade them for any amount of empty freedom."

"Uh..." Roz made a plaintive gesture.

"Rambunctious? Demanding? ...Noisy?"

Roz accepted this new word with a wry head-duck. After a little, he said, "I don't know any skill but robbing. And being a very poor soldier."

"Not true," said Pen. "I noticed you have quite a knack for counting and calculating. Something might be made of that, if you were given more tools."

"You mean learn to read."

"And write. But, you know, if you want an indoor job, sitting down, where you don't have to lie to or kill anyone, it's a direction to look. If that sounds good to you."

Put that way…it sounded wondrous. But… "How would I even start?"

"Well, most people start with letters and numbers." Pen picked up a stick, scraping his foot back and forth on the dirt to create a smooth surface. "I'm sure you know some already. Let's see how many…"

Polite, or maybe just Penric, of him not to say *Most* children *start with letters.* Drawn in despite himself, Roz began to attend. The work Pen made the letters do, squared up into their little road gangs of words, were well enough, dimly familiar. But the tricks he made the *numbers* do, sometimes pulling Roz's dice into play for help, were like nothing the old acolyte back at his home village had ever shown him, or even hinted existed. It was Penric, not Roz, who called a halt to this game at last to seek their bedrolls.

The next morning's ride on the winding road among the hills was strangely peaceful. Neither beast nor human lost any shoes. Their animals were unnaturally well behaved, all three now seeming smitten with the sorcerer, and Roz had an uncomfortable moment wondering if that uncanny effect also extended to road companions, and how he could tell. But better, no galloping soldiers came from behind shouting orders for the arrest of the dangerous thief. ...Either dangerous thief.

They came to the border posts between Oxousa and Orbas in the late afternoon. The Trigonie side was a shack for the recording clerk and tax collector, with a handful of soldiers to, mainly, raise the pole across the road and collect the small border fee, which Pen paid for them both without blinking. The contents of his cases, which he dubbed his personal library, were examined with as little understanding as Roz had first had, and passed without further comment. The inspecting soldier somehow became distracted before he came to Roz's saddlebags; Pen turned away dabbing a cloth to his nose, discreetly folding it around the red stain and pocketing it. Roz breathed again. He'd been pretty sure a perfectly true grunt of *Found it* would not have been accepted by the inspector asking where he'd come by his cache of coins. Undelayed, they remounted and ambled on down the road across a trickling ford.

At the lip of the shallow valley on the Orban side, a whole village lay, grown up around its larger post garrison and courier station. It held an inn, a blacksmith, a livery, and a large caravan compound to both serve and live off the passing travelers. Much the sort of place Roz used to scout for future victims, once. He didn't have to do that foul task today. Or ever again?

He braced himself for who-knew-what when they were held up by the barrier soldiers, and Penric, for the first time in Roz's hearing, gave his full name, *Learned Penric kin Jurald of Vilnoc.* With a wave at Roz he added only, "He's with me." It seemed to be all the document stamp required. One man scurried into the post building. In moments, an Orban captain in full summer uniform came hurrying back out, sword bobbing at his side and sandals slapping on the boardwalk.

"Learned Penric! You're back!" he cried, as if for a delight unforeseen.

"Hello again, Captain!"

"Did your journey prosper?"

"Yes, it did." Penric cast him down a cheery tally sign like a check-mark over his torso, more triumphant salute than blessing.

"No untoward snags, I hope?"

"None to speak of."

Penric and the BANDIT

Roz managed a stuffed smile, and didn't flinch.

"You were expected before this. Courier messages for you have been piling up. There's one from Duke Jurgo, and one from the archdivine in Dogrita, and one from your holy chapterhouse in Vilnoc. Ah, and one from your wife."

Having listened to the first part of this extraordinary roll call with a bored air, Pen suddenly brightened up. "Oh, I want that one!"

"Then come inside, learned sir, if you please…"

They slid off their saddles again. With a quick call over his shoulder to Roz of, "This won't take long. Look after the horses, if you'd be so kind," Pen followed the officer into the post building.

Both Roz and the two border soldiers stared after him. The soldiers looked…awed?

"You, ah, know him?" Roz prodded.

"Not to say *know*," denied the sergeant humbly. "I got to see him for the first time when he passed through here a week or so ago. Told my wife."

"Duke Jurgo's own court sorcerer!" his junior enthused. "He's known all over the world, they say, in his Order. Supposed to be the most powerful mage in Orbas, maybe the whole peninsula. And whip-smart, too. He's the sorcerer who led the army physicians, near a decade back, in wiping out the bruising-fever running through the ranks. That plague almost killed more men than a battle. The army still remembers *that*, you can bet on it." He nodded firmly. "Married to General Adelis Arisaydia's twin sister, too."

"That would be…the Red-Eyed General?" Roz said faintly.

"The Demon-Eyed General, his enemies called him, but that wasn't true," said the sergeant wisely. "It's his brother-in-law that has the famous demon. Have you really met her to talk to, traveling with the learned sir?"

"Desdemona? Er, yes, sort of."

Oohs of interest followed this statement. Before Roz could be interrogated further, Penric returned, folding a sheaf of papers and stuffing them in his tunic. He looked vastly cheerful.

"No bad news from home!" he told Roz. "Some other people think they have problems, but, really. If my trip was fruitful, which it was, I am urged, forcefully, to break our journey in Dogrita by the archdivine and the seminary's chief librarian in chorus. Which, since he's my supervisor's supervisor, I'd best take as an order. Planned to anyway—I expect to swap out my horse for a Temple coach there, with nice padded seats, which my hind end is ready for. Also, his curia keeps a generous table." He blinked at Roz. "You are, of course, also invited."

"As what?" said Roz blankly.

"Well now," said Penric, with a slow, sly smile. "That seems a question for you to answer." He jerked his head, leading Roz aside out of earshot of the soldiers.

"As your spiritual advisor I will remind you, you have made a tacit oath before the white god, Who always bears us witness, to commit no crime in Orbas. It would be a perilous promise to break. Otherwise, from here you are free to come with me, or to go anywhere else you please. With frugality and wit, I imagine you could make something starting with that seed corn in your saddlebags. Though I think you could make something better if you sell yourself less cheaply. So?"

Was this what *light of heart* felt like? It was a sensation so altogether new in Roz's experience, he could barely put a name to it. He drew breath. "I believe I'll follow you, for now," he said steadily. "Seeing as how you'll have me. Besides, it'd be a shame to miss your demon's next show. You two are sodding insane, you know that?"

The flash of a smirk—though from which of them, man or demon, Roz was not sure. The sorcerer, or was it the learned divine, nodded in serene satisfaction, and led back to their waiting mounts.

With growing curiosity Roz turned in Penric's wake, stepping toward his future self.